# Wishes of the Witch

Crypt Witch cozy paranormal mystery series - book 8

## K.E. O'Connor

K.E. O'Connor Books

# Chapter 1

The steady fall of rain from the slate-gray sky matched my sour mood. I tapped my fingers on the top of a bar that had seen better days and tried to ignore my rumbling stomach. I was overdue dinner.

Five days out of Willow Tree Falls, and I missed everything about my wonderful, quirky village. I missed Mom's cooking and her interference in my love life, my sister's endless supply of brownies, the chilled vibe in my bar, and Wiggles. I missed him stealing my pillows, eating all the food, and making wisecracks.

I checked the time again and sighed. Isaac Dubrov was half an hour late.

As the minutes dragged by, my irritation grew. I didn't appreciate being stood up.

"Another drink?" The dull-eyed bartender nodded at my empty glass.

"Sure. Same again."

He refilled my glass with soda water and a wedge of lime and slid it toward me. "Your date's not shown up?"

"He'd better," I muttered.

"If he suggested meeting here, it's probably best he's a no show."

"This place was my suggestion." I'd noticed the bar when staking out the pizza parlor across the road.

The demon I was hunting had gone there every day, and this was the perfect location to meet Isaac and watch my prey.

"Better luck next time." The bartender shrugged and walked away.

No matter what town or city I came to when I left Willow Tree Falls, they all felt the same. They lacked that sparkle of magic that gave my home its unique feel.

I glanced around the bar at the handful of other patrons. How could humans live like this? There didn't seem to be any joy as they rushed around with panic in their eyes.

It was illegal to use magic around humans. Although, I got a hall pass when I was hunting a demon. However, if I decided to go on vacation and accidentally blasted a human with a memory wipe spell, I'd be hauled in front of the Magic Council to explain myself.

Palak, the demon I was chasing, was currently gorging himself on a family-sized deep pan meat feast pizza. I could just make out his hunched back and claws through the steamed window. To humans, he looked like an average guy, but I saw straight through his disguise.

That meal would keep him occupied for a while, which was perfect. He could eat, while I got the information I needed.

Isaac Dubrov was a trader who specialized in illegal magic spells. He had his ear to the underground magic grapevine and got to hear all the secrets, which was why we were meeting. I hoped he knew something about my missing dad.

A finger prodded my shoulder. "Need some company, hot stuff?"

I turned in my seat, my gaze running over the tall, stocky guy dressed in dark jeans and a navy-blue T-shirt that had seen better days. "My own company's more than enough to keep me entertained."

His brows lowered for a second. "So, you're a clever one? Like to joke?"

"I have a terrible sense of humor." I turned away, hoping he'd get the hint.

"I love funny girls." He settled on the stool next to me.

"Then go find yourself one."

He snorted a laugh. "Can I get you a drink?"

"I'm sure you can. The question is, should you?"

His forehead wrinkled. "Does that mean you want one or not?"

My patience was hanging by its last thread. This guy had better not push me or it would snap. "Find someone else to chat to. I'm waiting on someone."

"Husband or boyfriend?" An eyebrow arched. "Or a girlfriend? I don't mind. We're equal opportunities here."

"None of the above," I said.

"So, you're single?"

I lifted my gaze to the ceiling. Top marks for persistence, but he'd picked the wrong day to mess with me. "You need to look elsewhere."

"I'm just seeking out some fun." His hand slid down my arm. "You've been sitting on your own for ages. You must be lonely."

"I promise you, I'm not."

He was quiet for a second. "You must have an Irish heritage with that black hair and pale skin. It's sexy."

I shrugged. "I like potatoes and Guinness, if that's what you mean."

"Potatoes? I don't get it. You want me to take you out for some french fries?"

I sighed softly. I doubt this guy got much. "I'm sure the woman of your dreams is out there waiting for you. I'm not her. I don't want company. I'm waiting for someone. Take the hint."

He grinned. "I love it when a girl plays hard to get."

I closed my eyes. That was it. Patience officially snapped. I dropped a couple of barriers inside me, just enough to let Frank slide up my spine and warm my insides. When I flicked my eyes open, I locked gazes with the guy and bared my teeth.

He jerked back in his seat as if he'd seen something terrifying. He stared at me without speaking for several seconds. "Erm. Uh. I mean... I just remembered I need to be somewhere." He practically ran out of the bar.

"That's enough for now," I muttered to Frank as I pushed him back down.

Frank grumbled a few times but was content to slide away. Since we'd been away from Willow Tree Falls, I'd given him a whole day out. He'd had the freedom to roam wherever he liked. It meant I'd woken one morning with a banging headache and a hazy memory of breaking into a bakery and gorging on triple chocolate brownies, but he was sated. He'd had his freedom fix, and he was a happy little demon.

It was a shame the same couldn't be said for this miserable little witch.

I picked up my glass and took a sip. I was tempted to try something stronger, but every alcoholic drink I'd sampled on previous visits always left a sour taste. It was nothing like the single malt dwarfen whiskey I served in Cloven Hoof. And nothing held a torch to my speciality lemon drops.

I placed money on the bar and stood. I was done wasting time.

As I turned to the door, it swung open.

Isaac strolled in. He stood at an imposing six-foot five, dressed in a knee-length black frock coat and black jeans. He looked like a chunky pirate.

His gaze flitted across the few people in the bar before settling on me. He nodded and scrubbed a hand across his stubbled chin.

I lifted my own chin in response as my eyes slid to the enormous scarlet and blue parrot on his right shoulder. Yep, he was definitely going for scary pirate today.

Isaac inclined his head to a table at the back of the bar.

I grabbed more drinks and followed him to the gloomy corner. I settled on the seat opposite him and passed him a glass. "Did you forget we were supposed to be meeting?"

A cold smile slid across his face as he stroked a finger down the parrot's chest. "Timekeeping never was my speciality. When there's business to be done, it always takes precedence."

"This isn't business?"

The sides of his mouth turned down. "I've yet to decide. I'm not sure what you've got to offer me, Tempest Crypt."

"She's a pretty one," the parrot said.

"As are all the Crypt witches," Isaac said. "This is Crimson Squawker. I've had him twenty years. He's my right-hand man, well, bird. I'd trust him with my life."

"Nice to meet you, Crimson," I said.

"Mr. Squawker to you," Isaac grumbled.

I took note of the bird's sharp talons. "Mr. Squawker it is. So, I need information."

Isaac's gaze ran over me. "I was intrigued to come and find out more. You're looking for your father?"

I nodded. Ever since Foxglove Shadowsoul announced she knew my dad was still alive, I'd been unsettled. I had to know if it was true.

When I got offered a freelance job by Angel Force to go demon hunting, it gave me the perfect opportunity to do some digging and see if there was any truth to Foxglove's statement.

"He's been missing for ten years," I said.

"What happened?"

"He just disappeared," I said. "He went out one day and never came back."

"Problems at home?"

"Nothing he wasn't handling," I said.

"Marriage problems?"

"No. He loved my mom. She was heartbroken when he left."

"Sometimes, people can act heartbroken to cover up something."

I scowled at him. "Not my mom. They loved each other. Sure, they argued now and again, but they had a good relationship. His disappearance had nothing to do with her."

"What about you?"

"You think I did something bad to my dad?"

Isaac's tongue poked out from between his teeth. "You're the demon carrier. You've had that demon since you were a kid, haven't you?"

"You seem to know a lot about me." I rubbed my forehead. It seemed like everyone knew the story about me swallowing a demon to protect my sister.

"I like unusual things, and I collect strange information." He grinned slowly. "What's stranger than you?"

"Thanks for the compliment. My demon's under control. And he didn't get his demon claws into my dad. The last time I saw him, he was in Willow Tree Falls. Aurora was rushing us out the door to get to school, and I was dragging my heels."

"You didn't like school?" Isaac grinned.

"Not much. I can imagine you weren't a grade A student, either. Anyway, Dad walked us to the end of the lane, and we split up. It wasn't until we were all sitting around the dinner table that night, and he still wasn't home, that we began to worry. The last anyone saw of him, he was walking toward the magic barrier."

"He was leaving the village?"

I nodded. "That's right."

"Did he have anything with him?"

"Nothing. He left everything behind. All he had were the clothes on his back and whatever was in his wallet."

"What are his powers?"

"Is that important?"

"Power can enhance, but it can also extinguish," Isaac said. "What's to say your dad didn't turn rogue and simply decide to leave Willow Tree Falls in search of something more... enticing?"

Those words hit home, and I winced. They were similar to what Foxglove had said. "He was a good dad to my sister and me. His powers weren't excessive. He was a mid-level warlock."

"Nothing special about him?"

My throat tightened. "Everything."

Isaac smirked. "I mean, any unusual ability that might draw attention? Maybe he has a skill somebody wanted to acquire. It's not outside the realm of possibility he was taken and is being forced to work for somebody against his will."

"Is that what you've heard?" I leaned closer. "When I contacted you, you said you knew something about him."

Isaac sipped his drink and grimaced. "What's this?"

"Water. We both need clear heads."

He gestured to the barman. "Whiskey sour."

I rapped a finger on the back of his hand. "My dad? What do you know?"

He waggled his head. "Before I tell you anything else, let's organize our trade."

"What do you want?" I was too quick to speak, but I was getting desperate for information. Every lead I'd been following had quickly vanished.

Isaac's grin was sharp. "Be careful not to offer too much. I always collect."

"Spit it out." I glowered at him.

He lifted his palms. "I require a small thing. The final ingredient for the spell of vanquishing."

I grimaced and shook my head. "That's not happening. I'm not trading dark magic with you. A spell like that would mean trouble for both of us. Besides, who do you want to vanquish?"

He lifted a shoulder. "A witch of your renown must know that spell."

"Even if I did, you're not getting the information."

"I figured as much. Every list of ingredients is missing one vital element. I've been attempting to complete that spell for some time. It would be most useful."

"And you plan to vanquish..."

He shook his head and tapped the side of his nose. "That's my secret to keep. If not that, then how about you give me use of your demon for one day?"

I choked out a laugh. "You have no idea what you're asking. Frank isn't controlled by anybody when he gets loose."

"Ha! I heard that you called him Frank. He must enjoy that cute nickname."

"It riles him. I do it for my own amusement." I said. "But I can't lend him to you. He's unpredictable and dangerous."

"Which is exactly what I need for the task I have in mind."

"Frank's off the table," I said. "Ask for something else."

Isaac twisted his mouth to the side. "There's nothing you can offer me."

I wasn't letting him go without finding out what he knew. "Maybe you have someone causing trouble in your life. I hunt demons for a living. Any demon problems you need me to sort out?"

He chuckled. "A lot of my dealings involve demons. I can't tarnish my reputation by openly associating with a Crypt witch to get rid of my enemies."

"It's already a terrible reputation," Crimson Squawker said.

Isaac grinned. "You mean terrifying. But if you can't get me the spell I require, and I can't make use of your demon services..."

We were silent as the barman brought over his drink.

Isaac took a sip. "There is a trivial matter you can assist with. It's hardly worth mentioning."

I was walking into a trap, but I went there anyway. "What is it?"

"Tell me about Angel Force."

My head jerked back. I hadn't expected that. "Angel Force? Why do you want to know about them?"

"They're a thorn in my side," he said. "They illegally took my precious supplies."

"They took things that can be used as evidence against you?"

"What they have will never be traced back to me," he said, "but I need it returned."

"What is it?"

"A few trifling objects. Nothing to concern yourself with," he said. "The less you know, the better. All I need is the layout of the Angel Force building."

"So you can steal what they've taken?"

"You can't steal something if it already belongs to you," Isaac said. "I simply need to know the easiest way to get in, so I can locate my items, remove them quietly, and leave without anybody noticing. Nobody will get hurt."

My eyes narrowed. I didn't trust Isaac, but I was desperate to hear anything about my dad. I'd been following supposed leads and dead ends for three months. All I was getting was frustrated and convinced that what Foxglove had told me was a lie. But I couldn't let it go, not until I knew for certain.

"It's a simple enough request, Tempest," Isaac said. "I believe you have dealings with the angels from time to time. Isn't your current mission to deal with Palak authorized by them?"

I lifted my chin. "How do you know that?"

He raised his hands. "I'm a gatherer of useful information and a trader of knowledge. I know you work with them. You must have been inside their building. Simply tell me how to get in and out and leave the rest to me."

I debated this request as I sipped on my drink. "You're not going to hurt the angels?" I wasn't their biggest fan, but I also didn't like to think they'd be injured if I gave out this information.

"Hand on my blackened heart, those angels will know nothing about me being there. I'll be quiet, stealthy, and invisible. Unless they check their evidence store, they won't even know what's missing. It's a simple request. Give me the information, and I'll tell you what I know about your dad."

"I'll do it. But I don't want to learn you've destroyed the place and taken the angels out while you were there."

He chuckled. "I didn't know you cared about them."

"We rub along well enough most of the time. But if it gets back to them that I've helped you with this, that goodwill will disappear." And Dazielle would have another reason to dislike me.

Isaac nodded. "This is between us. Tell me everything you know."

I spent five minutes giving him the lowdown on the angels' building. He listened intently, Crimson Squawker also paying attention as I mapped out the layout and the easiest way to get in the building without being noticed.

Although I'd never been in the angels' evidence store, I had a pretty good idea where it was. It wouldn't be difficult to get in and grab what he needed.

"That's everything I know," I said. "Now, tell me about my dad." My pulse kicked as I waited for him to speak.

Isaac's finger idly stroked down Crimson Squawker's chest. "He's keeping off grid."

"You've seen him?" My heart thudded.

"I haven't seen him. But after you contacted me, I did some asking around. I learned more of his history, which corroborates everything you've said. He left your village and has been trying to make himself invisible ever since."

"I already know that," I said. "I want recent details. Has anyone seen him since he left Willow Tree Falls?"

He nodded. "Six months ago in the dark realm."

I swallowed, my throat tightening. "Doing what?" The dark realm was no place for any decent magic user. It was a place for outcasts, those wanted by the law, and magic users who had no respect for the natural order. Dad would never go there.

"Why does anybody go into the dark realm?" Isaac asked. "It's the perfect place to become a nobody. People don't care what you do in there. There are no laws. Even the angels keep away because they won't survive five minutes in that place."

"You must have heard something about why he went in there."

"No idea," Isaac said. "I could make suggestions, but I'd have no evidence to back them up. The last confirmed sighting of him was six months ago."

"Anything could have happened in that time." My hands landed flat on the table. "You must have more information."

"Nothing else."

My frustration and anger alerted Frank. He zoomed up my spine and tickled the back of my neck.

Isaac's nostrils expanded, and Crimson Squawker screeched. "Steady now, Tempest. I understand this is a difficult time for you, but your papa must be staying away for a good reason."

"He can't be doing this willingly," I said. "Has he been seen with anyone shady? Have you heard that anyone's been using him?"

"No, nothing like that. As far as I can tell, he's not in servitude to anyone. He just doesn't want to be around people anymore. He left you and the rest of your family to be on his own. Maybe he simply preferred it that way."

The idea lodged in my gut like a cold hard ball of something toxic. I'd wondered this myself. Dad had given up on us. He'd walked away from his family because he wanted something more. Our weirdness and strange ways had been too much for him.

"How do I know I can trust you?" I asked.

"If I lied to people who asked me to get accurate information, I wouldn't be alive and talking to you." Isaac's eyes blazed with indignation. "My word is my oath. I promise you, that's all the information I could find. My source is accurate."

"Who's your source? I have to meet them."

He waved a finger in the air. "No, that's not how we do things. I have my own connections within the community. I make use of them. You don't get to do that. Anything you need, you come through me. And if you want to validate what I'm saying, then go see your dad for yourself."

I raked a hand through my hair. I had no plans to go anywhere near the dark realm unless it was a last resort. People who went in often didn't come out. "That's all you've got to tell me?"

"For now," he said. "But you were generous with your information about the angels. I'll continue to seek reliable leads about your father. But he's been gone a long time and is doing an excellent job of keeping hidden. Have you thought that perhaps he's doing it for your benefit?"

"How is not having him around helping me?"

"He could have left because there was a problem he didn't want to inflict upon his family."

"Dad wouldn't do that," I said. "And he didn't have any problems big enough to make him walk away from us. We'd have helped, whatever it was. It can't be that."

Isaac's gaze lifted over my shoulder. "Well, that's all I can tell you. And if you want to catch that demon you're hunting, you need to get a wiggle on. He's about to make his move on a cute blonde. It would be a tragedy to see that pretty face spoiled because you got distracted on your mission."

I stood from my seat and stared through the grimy window of the bar. Sure enough, Palak was lurking in the shadow outside the door of the pizza parlor. The cute blonde in question was oblivious to his presence as she chatted on her phone and twirled a curl around one finger.

"One more thing. I..." I looked back at Isaac. His seat was empty. The only thing that remained was a single red feather from Crimson Squawker.

I stomped out of the bar, my demon target in sight and my anger blazing. This was just what I needed, a knockdown fight with a demon. I had to take my frustration out on something. What better than a misbehaving demon with cheese stuck to his chin?

And once I'd captured Palak, I needed to figure out my next move when it came to finding my dad.

What was he doing in the dark realm? And how was I going to get him back?

# Chapter 2

"I've got such amazing news." Aurora skipped through my apartment door, her blonde hair bouncing and a smile lighting her face.

I shuffled around the kitchen counter, still in my slippers and dressing gown. I yawned loudly as I flicked on the kettle. "I'm happy for you, whatever it is." Her loud knocking on my door hadn't been the best way to be woken.

Aurora placed her purse on the counter. Bandit, her newly acquired familiar, in the loosest sense of the word, poked her ginger head out.

"What's she doing here?" Wiggles growled at Bandit.

Bandit ignored him. She hopped on the counter and strutted around, sniffing the fruit bowl as she passed by.

"I bring her everywhere." Aurora booped Bandit on the nose.

Bandit rubbed around her hand and purred. "As her ideal familiar, I never leave her side."

I pulled my messy bed hair off my face. "So, what brings you here so early?"

Aurora grinned as she settled at the counter and pulled out a plastic container full of brownies. "Lots of reasons. But first, what's up with you?"

"I've been working overtime hunting a demon," I said. "Coffee?"

"Yes, please." She opened the plastic box, and the delicious smell of dark chocolate lifted my mood a fraction. "Was this one particularly difficult?"

"They're all difficult," I said.

"But you got him? There were no problems?"

"No more than usual." I made two coffees and settled at the counter with Aurora.

She handed me a brownie. "Well, that's one of the reasons I'm here. You were gone almost a week. I missed my favorite sister."

"I'm your only sister," I mumbled around a mouthful of brownie.

"Same thing," she said. "Anyway, I missed you. I also wanted you to try my new brownie recipe. What do you think?"

"Delicious." I tried not to spray brownie crumbs everywhere. "What else?"

"Tell them about the castle," Bandit whispered.

My eyebrows lifted. "Castle Falls? What about it? Has there been another fire? Or have the ghosts finally destroyed it so no one can ever move in?"

"It has a new owner," Bandit said before Aurora had a chance to speak. "When I heard the news, I thought it was a joke. I'm still having night terrors from the time we found Trixie tied up there and Foxglove tried to kill us."

"Is this true?" I asked Aurora.

"Very true," she said. "And, the new owner's ridiculously wealthy and very handsome."

"Oh, I get now why you're happy. You're finally back to husband hunting." It had taken Aurora a good six months to get over being duped by her fiancé and having him turn her into a stone dragon.

But the last few weeks, she'd gained a more appreciative eye for the opposite sex again. And it looked like the new owner of Castle Falls would be her next target. Poor guy.

"He's so cute," she said on a sigh. "Movie star gorgeous with a sprinkle of magic to make him even yummier."

"You've met him?" I asked.

"Met him! He spent all afternoon in my store yesterday. He's charming, with old school manners. And he dresses like a real gentleman."

"Hold on a second." I lifted a hand. "You said a lot of those things about Toby."

"We don't mention that horrible name," she said. "I made an error in judgment over him. However, Lex Fontaine's different from Toby. He has generations of excellent manners bred into him. And he has a lovely accent and a deep voice. My toes curl whenever he talks."

"And what did you do all afternoon in your store?" I arched an eyebrow.

"Flirted outrageously," Bandit said.

"He did not," Aurora said.

"I meant you," Bandit said.

Her cheeks flushed bright pink. "Well, I may have been a little over-friendly, but there's something about him that makes me giggle like a school girl."

I groaned. "Please don't tell me you've fallen in love with him. Get to know this guy first. Go out on lots of dates and grill him about everything. Whatever you do, don't let him charm you. Besides, isn't your 'too good to be true' alarm pinging about him?"

"Why would it be?"

"What's a hot, rich guy doing unmarried? If he's as amazing as you claim, he must have women chasing after him, desperate to get their toes curled too."

She pursed her lips. "Shows what you know. He probably has lots of female attention, but here's the sad thing about his life. He was widowed two years ago. Apparently, his wife was a real beauty. She had long, flowing white hair and purple eyes."

"White hair and purple eyes? She sounds like a jinn descendant."

"Correct," Aurora said. "As is he. Both are direct descendants of jinns."

Wiggles bounced up and down and slammed his paws against the kitchen cabinet. "Which means he can grant wishes. Whatever we want is ours."

"Hold your fluffy paws," I said. "It's not that simple. If he does have the ability to grant wishes, he'd never leave his lamp out for anyone to rub. Otherwise, he'd be inundated with people desperate to grab their three wishes and make their dreams come true."

"It's like my dream has already come true," Aurora said on a contented sigh. "He's such a gorgeous guy. The perfect guy for me."

I wrinkled my nose and shared an amused grin with Wiggles. Aurora was finally over Toby and moving on. A part of me was glad, but it also meant I'd have to endure her simpering over her latest crush.

She continued to extol Lex's virtues as I finished my brownie and drank my coffee.

Should I tell her about my investigation into our dad? I still had nothing concrete to go on. If I revealed what I was doing, and it came to nothing, she'd only be disappointed, and she'd had enough of that in her life.

No, I was keeping this to myself for now. Not even Wiggles knew what I was up to, and I shared everything with him.

"So, are you interested?" Aurora asked.

My focus had drifted from the conversation after she'd described the type of tie Lex had been wearing when he paid her a visit. "What's that?"

She tutted. "Will you go visit Lex?"

"Me? I thought you were the one who wanted to marry him?"

She slapped the back of my hand. "Let's not talk about marriage, not just yet, anyway. You're what Lex needs right now. That's the reason he came to my store."

"Because of me?"

"Yes! You haven't been listening to a word I said."

"I heard most of it," I said. "Crazy, rich guy buys destroyed castle for some unknown reason and hung out in your store yesterday and charmed you."

"Why do you think he's crazy?" she asked.

"Because he bought Castle Falls," I said, "the most haunted place in the whole universe."

"Don't be silly. There might be one or two ghosts in the castle, but that's it. Well, and possibly a demon."

I sucked in a breath. "Why do you say that?"

She rolled her eyes. "I don't know why I bother with you. That's why Lex wants to see you. He thinks his castle has a demon in it. He wants you to hunt it down for him."

I sat up straight. "A demon! Is he sure?"

"He's not sure what's going on, but Lex is really worried. I could tell he hadn't slept well in days when he came to Heaven's Door," she said. "I gave him sleeping drafts and some magic to assist, but he needs professional help in rooting out the problem."

"If there's a demon on the loose in Willow Tree Falls, we'd know," I said. "Lex must have made a mistake. It could be just an annoying poltergeist keeping him up at night."

"He's convinced there's something dark in that castle." Her blue eyes narrowed. "Don't go messing up my chances with him by turning down this job."

"Come off it. It won't be my fault if you can't get it on with Mr. Super-Rich."

"It won't help if you say no to this job." She grabbed my hand. "Please, Tempest. Let's go to the castle and take a look around. It can't do any harm."

"And if we do, it means you get to hang out with Mr. Toe Curler again."

She shrugged. "It hadn't crossed my mind, but what a bonus."

"Do I have to come?" Bandit asked.

"Ha! You're such a scaredy cat," Wiggles said.

"Foolish hellhound," she sneered down at him. "You haven't forgotten the mad-eyed ghost who shoved you down the stairs the last time you were there, have you?"

"That ghost was aiming for you," Wiggles said. "And we all survived."

"Only just," Bandit muttered.

"We should all go," Aurora said. "We can make it a family outing. Besides, I heard Lex has already done a lot of restoration work to the castle."

"How's that possible? I've only been away five days."

"He bought the castle two months ago and has had a crew working on it since then," Aurora said. "He's just moved in. I bet the ghosts are thrilled with him being there and making their home beautiful."

"Don't set your expectations too high," I said. "That's one spooky place, and some of those ghosts are grumpy."

"Then you need to make it less spooky," she said. "I won't take no for an answer. Lex wants you to hunt a demon, and I agree with him."

I grabbed another brownie and took a bite. "Then it looks like we're going demon hunting."

# Chapter 3

"I was hoping for a break before I started my next demon hunt." I dragged my feet as I followed Aurora up the hill to Castle Falls.

"Why wait?" she said. "As soon as I contacted Lex to let him know you would take a look around the castle, he begged for you to come straight away."

I scowled, not happy to be returning to Castle Falls. The rumors about the ghosts haunting the place were true, and I'd had an unfortunate encounter with one the last time I'd been here. The ghost had claws and had screamed so loud my ears had rung for days.

Still, this made Aurora happy, and she deserved some of that in her life.

My eyes widened as we grew closer to the castle. "Wow! He's restored the turrets already."

She chuckled. "I told you Lex was wealthy. That was the first job he wanted done. He said he needed everything watertight and returned to its former glory, turrets included."

"More money than sense if you ask me," Wiggles said. "Think of all the pizzas you could buy with the money spent on those turrets. Who needs a turret these days, anyway?"

"A mad scientist who keeps his experiments locked away, so no one can discover them? Someone who has a wife possessed by a demon and doesn't want shame coming to the family name?" I suggested.

"How about a jinn looking to hide his magic lamp, so no one can rub it and get their wishes?" Wiggles said.

Aurora shook her head as she tucked a hand through my elbow. "Or someone who has a respect for the past and wants to make himself a beautiful home. Less dawdling. We have an appointment we can't be late for."

We stopped outside the imposing front entrance of the castle. Where there had once been nothing but a broken wooden door and the charred remains of the fire that had wrecked the castle was an imposing set of sturdy double doors.

Before we'd even had a chance to knock, the door was opened.

"Lex!" Aurora smiled brightly as she stepped forward.

"Aurora. So good to see you again. I'm glad you could make it." Lex Fontaine was classically handsome. His dark hair was streaked with white and swept off his elegant cheekbones, and his blue eyes were rimmed with a deep purple. He wasn't a bad-looking guy. Not my type, but I could see why he appealed to Aurora.

"This is my sister, Tempest." Aurora gestured to me.

I shook hands with Lex. "I've heard about the work on the castle. It's a huge undertaking."

He patted a stone wall. "I wanted a challenge. As soon as I saw this magnificent place, I knew this was what I was looking for."

"Why are you looking for a challenge?" I asked.

Aurora glared at me. "Shall we come in?"

"Of course!" Lex stepped aside and gestured us through the doorway.

Aurora didn't hesitate walking through, but I stood at the entrance and peered inside.

"I hear you've been here before," Lex said. "Your work assisting the angels sounds exciting."

"I wouldn't call it that," I said. "This place looks... really good." Gone were the soot stains and charred tapestries. Everything was clean and bright. Expensive looking furniture sat around, making the place look more like a home than a hotel for angry ghosts.

I glanced at Wiggles, and he nodded. "Let's take a look around."

Lex let out a sigh. "I do appreciate you coming so quickly." He walked by my side through the large stone entrance and into a huge hallway with high stained glass windows.

"I'll be honest. I didn't have much choice. Aurora can be persuasive when she wants something." I watched my sister coo over all the cute, no doubt outrageously expensive, ornaments lining the hallway.

He smiled, affection crossing his face as his gaze fixed on Aurora. "Your sister's charming. I walked into her store yesterday, and it felt like I was coming home. She was warm and welcoming, and she took my concerns seriously. As soon as she heard I had problems with a demon, she suggested I see you straightaway."

"Yeah, she's kind like that," I said.

Aurora stopped ahead of us and turned. "Lex, why don't you give us the grand tour? You can point out any areas of concern you have to my sister, and she can work her magic."

My gaze was full of warning as I caught her eye. There was no guarantee I'd be able to fix this problem Lex was having.

"That's a fine idea," he said. "So long as that's suitable for you, Tempest?"

I nodded. "Usually, if you have a problem with a demon, I'll be able to sense it. Some of them can be sneaky, though. It won't do any harm to have a look around to see if anything pops."

I glanced around as footsteps approached. A slender guy with delicately pointed ears, wearing large dark-framed glasses and dressed in dusty work overalls came out of a side room. His skin was luminous, and his beautiful green eyes marked him as an elf.

He slowed as he saw us. "Oh! I didn't know you had guests."

Lex gestured him over. "It's not a problem. Gregor Mornelis, these are my new friends, Aurora and Tempest Crypt. They're helping with the little... concern I have."

Gregor's dark green intelligent eyes moved from me to Aurora, and he nodded a greeting. "I'm glad to hear it."

"You've seen the demon?" I asked.

His eyes widened. "No! But I've been working here for months. It's a unique property."

"Gregor's my renovation expert," Lex said. "He's looking after the team of builders who are bringing this place back to glory."

"And you've seen unusual things while you've been here?" I asked. "I've heard ghosts don't like their environment disturbed. I imagine this building work is doing a lot of disturbing."

Gregor ran a hand through his messy dark hair. "We're not helping. Every time we knock down a wall, dig into the foundations, or erect scaffolding, we have an audience."

"They don't cause you problems, do they?" Aurora asked. "I've heard strange stories about the ghosts in this castle."

"They don't worry me. It's not my first encounter with ghosts," Gregor said. "And they normally hate it when you disturb the place where they live. But these ghosts simply seem curious. They stand around as if they're watching a play. At first, it was unsettling. On one occasion, we had fifteen ghosts watching us work, but they don't do anything."

"And it's not the ghosts I have concerns about," Lex said quietly.

"Are you certain it's not a ghost causing the problems?" I asked. "Spirits can be malevolent if they're not happy about something."

"If this is a ghost, it's the scariest one I've encountered," Lex said. "This haunting, or whatever it is, is full of malice."

Gregor cleared his throat. "I was going to go over the latest design sketches for the family room with you, but I see now's not a good time. Shall I leave them on your desk?"

"Thanks, that'll be great," Lex said.

Gregor smiled at us before hurrying away.

"Does Gregor know all about your demon issue?" I asked.

"I'm afraid so. I'm not sure he believes me, but he knows I'm troubled," Lex said. "You'll see him around most days. He lives on site. I had to have him here as soon as I bought this castle. He's an expert in renovating historical properties. Let me show you some of what he's already done."

He led us into a grand living room, with expensive, yet tasteful furniture. As we continued the tour, and he explained his plans, Aurora stared up at him with a worrying look of rapture in her eyes. She never learned to take her time with a guy.

I focused on sensing a demon. I couldn't feel anything malevolent in the castle, but there was a low-level sense of creepiness. Maybe it was just my experience of being in this place and almost getting killed that filtered through me, but something felt off.

Wiggles nudged me with his nose. "Check out this collection of lamps." He trotted to a glass cabinet containing a dozen tarnished bronze lamps.

They were backlit, and each had a hand-engraved plaque next to it with a different name on it.

"Those were my ancestors," Lex said as he approached the case.

"You're a descendent of jinns?" I said.

"That's correct. Our lineage goes back thousands of years. There's even some who claim we're the original genie lineage." Pride filtered through his words.

"I bet you get a lot of women who want to rub you because of that," Aurora said.

Lex coughed into his hand. "I do enjoy a good rub now and again."

I held in a laugh and raised my eyebrows at her. Aurora was anything but subtle when she liked a guy.

Her eyes widened as she clapped a hand over her mouth. "Oh! That sounded terrible. I didn't mean that. I meant, not that I'm sure you aren't lovely to rub, but because of your history. People must assume you can grant them wishes." She shot an anxious glance at me, but there was no way I was saving her from this hilarity.

Lex ducked his head, a gentle smile on his face. "I have had some interesting proposals over the years. But I'm not that kind of jinn."

"Of course, he's going to say that," Wiggles muttered.

"You don't have the ability to grant wishes?" I asked.

"The power faded as the magic diluted over time," Lex said. "Jinns fall in love with other magic users, and we have families. The wish power isn't so strong. I'm not without my abilities, but it's not of the wish granting variety. Unlike my ancestor, Sterling Fontaine. He was a magnificent genie. That's his lamp right at the end."

"What would you wish for if you had three wishes?" Aurora asked me.

"I know what I'd wish for," Wiggles said. "An unlimited amount of belly rubs, an endless supply of pizza, and..."

Bandit's head poked out of the large purse slung over Aurora's shoulder. "An end to your hideous gas problems?"

He grunted. "Maybe I'd wish you'd never been born."

Lex shook his head. "No negative wishes allowed. Only positive wishes are permitted."

"I didn't know that," Aurora said. "So, if I wanted to harm someone, not that I do, you'd deny me the wish?"

"There are gray areas when it comes to wishes," he said. "If you wanted to end the life of somebody who was harming others, that would be up for negotiation. It would be looked into to see if the wish should be granted. However, I'm not unhappy that I don't have the burden of wish giving. It's a difficult business. And often, people who have their wishes granted aren't happy with the outcome."

"I'd be happy with unlimited belly rubs and pizza," Wiggles said.

"Simple needs for a simple mind," Bandit said.

"Why don't you disappear back into your purse?" Wiggles grumbled before stomping away.

"Let me show you around the rest of the castle," Lex said. "You have yet to see the upstairs."

The next hour was spent looking around dozens of rooms. Many were empty, but all evidence of the fire and disrepair had gone.

I spotted a few ghosts as we wandered around, but they weren't interested in us.

"Where in the castle have you seen this demon?" I asked.

Lex rubbed the end of his nose. "My bedroom mainly and outside."

"What's it doing when you see it?"

"She disturbs my sleep," he said.

"The demon's a female?" That was rare, but I'd met a few female demons in my time.

"She is. She whispers to me and screams. I mainly see her outside the castle, though. I always get the sense she's watching me."

"Any idea why this demon might be interested in you?" I asked.

"She hasn't told me, but she does whisper to me when I'm asleep."

"What sort of thing does she say?"

Lex ducked his head and clasped his hands in front of him.

"Why don't we stop and have a coffee?" Aurora said. "All this walking around has made my feet ache."

"Of course! I've been so distracted by this demon problem that I sometimes forget myself. I'll ring for refreshments." He strode back into the main hallway and pulled a large corded rope hanging in the corner. "This is a wonderful invention. Some of them aren't working, but you pull this and a bell rings in the kitchen. It's so old-fashioned, but I couldn't get rid of the system. It would be a disservice to history."

A moment later, a middle-aged woman dressed in black with an apron tied around her middle appeared. "You rang, Mr. Fontaine?"

"Martha, we'd like refreshments in the living room," he said.

"Very good, Sir." She turned and hurried away.

"Martha came with me when I purchased this place." He led us into the living room, and we all settled on the couches. "She's been in my service for almost ten years. She wasn't certain she wanted to work in a haunted castle, but when I doubled her pay, she decided she could put up with the ghosts. I couldn't be without her."

Once the refreshments had been served, and I was sipping on some of the smoothest coffee I'd ever tasted, I headed back to the question of the demon.

"I understand talking about the demon makes you uncomfortable, but anything you can tell me will be helpful. I need to figure out what kind of demon she is, why she's here, and what she means to do to you, if anything."

"Do you think the demon means to hurt Lex?" Aurora grabbed his hand.

"I can't tell you," I said. "Sometimes, demons are simply annoying. They get pleasure out of irritating people."

He shook his head. "No. It's more than that. This feels personal."

"Why do you say that?" I asked.

Lex tugged at his bottom lip. "The demon knows things about me that very few people do. She's whispered about secrets of my childhood and problems I've had with business ventures, the kind of thing only someone close to me would know."

"Like an employee?" I asked. "Do you trust all your employees?"

"I do."

"Have you had to fire anyone who might be holding a grudge?" I asked. "Someone who might have the power to set a demon on you?"

Lex shook his head. "I've had to let a few people go over the years, but it's always been on decent terms. I'm good to the people I hire. I don't think it's that."

"If this demon isn't causing problems other than sleepless nights, maybe it's something you'll just have to learn to live with," I said.

Aurora shook her head as she set her cup down. "It's more serious than that."

"Serious how?" I watched the loaded glance that passed between Aurora and Lex.

Aurora nodded at him. "You can trust Tempest."

Lex licked his lips. "Go ahead. You may tell her."

"This demon is encouraging Lex to do bad things," she said.

"What kind of bad things?" I asked.

Lex's head dipped again.

Aurora clasped his hand between hers. "The demon's telling him to harm himself. Every night this week, she's whispered in his ear, encouraging him to go to the top of the castle and throw himself over the edge."

My eyebrows shot up. "While that's a horrible thing to have to hear, don't listen to her. Problem solved."

"It's not as easy as that," Aurora said. "This demon's influencing Lex to believe that's exactly what he should do."

He nodded. "I'm ashamed to say that I believe her. The last three nights, I've had Gregor chain me to the bed, so I can't move. The demon talks to me all night about how worthless I am and I should give up the fight. She tells me I'm pathetic and will never achieve what I want to do. She's convincing me that I should end things."

I sipped my coffee. "This demon has a real issue with you. Have you tried to speak directly to her?"

"Never. She always comes to me when I'm asleep, and she talks until I wake," he said. "The only times I see her when I'm awake is out in the grounds. She's too far away to talk to."

"What does she look like?" I asked.

"She shimmers," Lex said. "She has a pale haze around her, so it's hard to see her features. I'm sure it's some kind of disguise in case I recognize her. Not that I think I would. I don't think I've ever encountered a demon."

"You will in Willow Tree Falls," I said. "We have plenty of half-demons around here."

"Of course, and I have no issue with them," Lex said. "I don't want to give up on this castle, but I might have to do just that if I can't get rid of her."

"Have you only encountered her since moving here?" I asked.

His head tilted back, and he slumped onto the couch as if the fight had faded from him. "No, but she was less invasive. She'd talk to me sometimes, but I'd convinced myself it was my imagination.

I'd have vivid dreams and imagine someone was whispering in my ear, but then it would disappear, and I'd hear nothing for months."

"And it's only since coming here that she's stepped up her attention?" I said. "I wonder why."

His jaw wobbled as his gaze settled on me. His expression was one of anxiety and despair. This was a man on the edge.

"Tempest, do you think you can help Lex?" Aurora asked. "It's so unfair what's happening to him."

I looked around the room. "I've sensed nothing since I've been here. It'll need further exploration. And there's no guarantee I'll be able to stop this demon if I find her. It sounds like she can come and go at will, and if she's getting inside your subconscious while you sleep, that's territory I can't go into."

Lex stood, dropped to his knees, and grabbed my hands. "I beg you. Anything you can do to help, I'll agree to it. I feel like I'm losing my mind."

I patted his shoulder, uncomfortable at having Lex kneeling at my feet like he was about to make a marriage proposal. "I'll do what I can."

A sob choked out of him. "I've nowhere else to turn."

"Tempest!" Aurora hissed as she gestured at Lex.

I shrugged. I'd never had a guy beg at my feet before. This was a new and unpleasant experience. "How about I come back tomorrow night? I can stay overnight and do some reveal spells, see if I can kick up any interest from the demon."

He kissed the back of my hand. "I will be forever in your debt if you rid me of this demon."

I gently pulled my hand away and glanced at Aurora. I tried not to laugh as jealousy sparked in her eyes. She had to know I wasn't interested in this guy.

"This village is my home," I said. "No demon will cause problems while I'm living here."

"Anything you need," Lex said, "I'm at your disposal. Resources, magic, demon trapping equipment. I don't know what you use, but just ask, and I'll get it for you. Together, we will defeat this demon."

I nodded as I drank more coffee, and Lex returned to his seat. I had no idea if we could defeat this demon. The only thing I knew for sure was that I was about to go hunting demons in my own territory.

This could get interesting.

# Chapter 4

"We'll be fine with just the three of us this evening." Merrie Noble, my bar manager, gestured to two other bar staff before waving me toward the door. "Go enjoy your demon hunt at the castle."

I grimaced. "I'm only doing this to keep Aurora happy. Every time she's around this Lex guy, she lights up."

"I'm glad she's moving on," Merrie said. "We all love Aurora and hate what happened to her. Perhaps Lex is just what she needs."

"I'm not letting her spend too much time with him if he's really being bothered by a demon," I said. "Demons seem to like my sister."

"If there's a demon there, you'll deal with it," she said. "Any problems, I know where you are. We should have a quiet night, though."

After a final look around the bar, I nodded and headed out with Wiggles.

"You know when we do stakeouts," Wiggles said, "and we have all our supplies with us?"

I had a feeling I knew where this conversation was going. "How often have we done stakeouts?"

"Loads of times. I can't count the number of times on my paws."

"You're exaggerating," I said. "What supplies do you think we need? I've got my spell book and a few herbs. I'm not pulling out the big magic guns on this project just yet."

"A few of Brogan's triple cheese and bacon subs with some fries and cherry muffins is just what we need."

"You're planning to tempt the demon out with food?" I said. "Good idea."

He snorted a cloud of sulfur rich smoke. "I was thinking food for us. Staying awake all night requires energy. How's a hellhound supposed to operate if his stomach's growling? My gut grumbles might prevent you from hearing the demon sneaking up on you. If you die because I'm hungry, you'll only have yourself to blame."

I lifted a hand. "Food's not a bad idea. Let's see what Brogan's got on offer this evening."

We strode the short distance to Unicorn's Trough and headed inside.

Brogan had just finished serving a customer and turned to me with a smile as I approached the counter. "How's everything with my favorite Crypt witch this evening?" His shirt sleeves were rolled up, showing a fine pair of muscular arms covered in tattoos.

"So, I'm your favorite Crypt witch?" I said. "You'd better not let Granny Dottie hear you say that. She might curse you."

He chuckled. "You're all my favorite when you come here for food. What will it be?"

"We're on a mission tonight," Wiggles said. "We need fuel and plenty of it."

Amusement sparkled in Brogan's dark eyes. "What kind of mission?"

"One we need to be discreet about." I glared at Wiggles. "Although, it's not exactly a secret. Have you met the new owner of Castle Falls?"

"Of course. He moved in officially about a week ago, didn't he?" Brogan said.

"That's right," I said. "Lex Fontaine."

"Gotcha. He came here a few weeks ago and bought most of my food for a work crew he had on site for a few days. He left a generous tip as well. I'm happy to have him move to the village if he's going to help my business."

"He's also visited Aurora's store," I said. "Lex has an issue with the castle."

"The hauntings, you mean?" Brogan asked. "I can't imagine it's peaceful living in a place with so many ghosts."

Wiggles shook his head. "It's not ghosts; it's—"

"We're not sure what it is," I said. Lex wouldn't want his demon problem gossiped about. "That's why I'm heading over there tonight to see if we can unearth anything spooky."

Brogan's thick eyebrows lowered. "If you're involved, it's got something to do with demons."

"It's got more to do with my sister," I said. "She took a shine to Lex when he was in the store. She wants to make a good impression."

"Lucky him," Brogan said. "Your sister's a sweetheart."

"I didn't know you were interested in Aurora."

He grinned. "I might be if I was available."

"I didn't think you were seeing anyone. You've always told me you're not the settling type."

Brogan shrugged. "Things change. Maybe I've met someone who's convinced me that settling's the right thing to do."

I never thought I'd see the day when Brogan Costin was tamed by a woman. He was a flirt and always got Auntie Queenie hot under the collar whenever she saw him, but he was quick to move on from a relationship before it got intense.

He enjoyed the ladies but liked to keep his options open. And, with his striking dark looks inherited from his vampire ancestry, he always had plenty of attention.

"Are you going to tell me who she is?" I asked.

He lifted his shoulders. "I never kiss and tell."

"Do I know her? Does she live in the village?"

He mimed zipping his lips shut. "When she's ready for our relationship to go public, you'll be one of the first to know."

"How long have you been together?"

He shook his head and crossed his arms over his broad chest. "That's all you're getting from me, Tempest. Now, what do you need before you go on your epic demon hunting mission?"

I studied Brogan's face. He looked happy. There was a glow to him. Had Brogan fallen in love with this mystery woman?

I placed our food order and waited at the end of the counter, sipping on a complimentary coffee.

The door behind me opened.

Brogan lifted his head, and a smile lit his face. "You're earlier than I expected."

Two tall, elegant, clearly ancient vampires glided toward the counter.

"Your grandmother grew bored looking at the sculptures," the male vampire said.

These were Brogan's grandparents? I took a closer look. They radiated primordial power. It was a vibe often given out by vampires who'd seen a lot of life.

"The artist had an unsteady eye," she said. "Besides, I've seen so many sculptures that I grew weary. I'm not just here to enjoy the local culture. I want to spend as much time as possible with my grandson." She reached up with a pale, flawless hand and patted Brogan's cheek.

He grinned and glanced at me. "Tempest, I don't think you've met my grandparents."

I walked over and set my coffee down. "Can't say I have."

"Tempest Crypt, this is Granny Ana and Grandpa Cezar."

Grandpa Cezar bowed, and Granny Ana inclined her head toward me.

"They're visiting for a week," Brogan said.

"Nice to meet you both," I said.

Granny Ana's cool, dark gaze ran over me. There was always something ever so slightly creepy about vampires. They had an unnatural beauty that I always wanted to prod to see if it was truly as flawless as it looked.

"Of the Crypt witch lineage," she finally said once she'd finished studying me like I was an intriguing specimen in a zoo. "Your ancestors have quite a reputation."

"I hope it's not just my ancestors," I said. "Those of us who are alive do okay."

A flicker of a smile traced across Granny Ana's face. "Indeed, you do. You guard us against the demons."

"And Tempest is a demon swallower." Brogan placed my food order on the counter.

Granny Ana moved so fast I barely had time to flinch before she was nuzzling against my neck as she inhaled deeply.

Wiggles growled and bared his teeth.

I lifted a hand to let him know I wasn't being drained of blood just yet.

Brogan cleared his throat. "Granny, remember, not everyone's used to being around our family. Move slower, so as not to startle Tempest."

My pulse thudded, screaming a warning that there was a vampire close to an important vein in my neck. If she bit me, we'd have a battle on our hands, one I wasn't certain I'd win.

Grandpa Cezar stepped forward and gently touched his wife's arm. "My dear, remember yourself." His eyes flashed me an apology. "You smell most intriguing, Tempest."

Granny Ana finally glided back, guided by her husband. Her gaze latched onto mine, and her tongue traced across her bottom lip. "When we entered the café, I sensed a delicious combination of supernatural ability."

"You can smell Frank?" I asked.

Her head cocked like a startled bird. "Your demon is called Frank?"

"That's what I call him. Does he smell good to you?" My hand moved to the place on my neck where she'd sniffed.

"It's a unique combination," she said. "I grow tired of the familiar smells and tastes available to us. To find something new, it's like discovering a new flavor of ice cream. You have to indulge."

I glanced at Wiggles, who was still rumbling a warning deep in his chest and took a step back. "I don't want you indulging in me. I like my blood to stay in my veins."

"Granny," Brogan said, a note of warning in his voice, "we've talked about this. You're here to enjoy the peace and quiet in Willow Tree Falls, not find a new meal to enjoy."

A shudder ran down my spine. Vampires were discreet and usually well-behaved when it came to finding their food. They weren't permitted to feed in the village, or should I say, on the villagers. It was against the law to take a chomp out of anyone who didn't willingly submit. Even so, a shiver of unease ran through me.

The intense curiosity on Granny Ana's face faded. She gently shook her head as she clasped her hands together. "May I offer you a thousand apologies? My actions were most unnecessary."

"My wife means no harm," Grandpa Cezar said. "When you've lived as long as we have, it's hard to find much to stimulate you. Everything looks like it's changing, but in truth, it remains the same. Ana has always been passionate about smells. She loves to explore anything new. Neither of us mean you harm. And since you're a friend of our grandson's, you come under our care."

"You do," Granny Ana said.

I glanced at Brogan, and he nodded. "Everything's good here, Tempest. You can trust them."

"I guess I should take it as a compliment that I smell so tasty," I said.

Hunger flared in Granny Ana's eyes as she stared at me.

Oops! That was totally the wrong thing to say. It was time to leave before the vampires changed their minds.

I grabbed the food and handed Brogan some money.

He shook his head and pushed it away. "On the house."

"You don't have to do that," I said.

He looked at his grandparents, who still eyed me like I was an all you can eat buffet. "Yes, I do. Enjoy your evening."

I wasn't going to hang around and argue. Clutching the food to my chest, I nodded goodbye to Brogan's grandparents and hurried out.

"That was mildly disturbing," Wiggles said.

"It's always the same with ancient vampires," I muttered. "Silent, deadly, and terrifying. Come on. Let's see if we can make ourselves even more terrified by spending the night in a haunted castle."

# Chapter 5

My pulse no longer thudded a warning to flee as I put distance between the vampires and me and entered Castle Falls.

I looked around, expecting to find Lex, but he was nowhere to be seen.

Footsteps approached, and I spotted Gregor.

He raised a hand as he sped toward me. "Sorry, I was supposed to be here to meet you. Lex is dealing with some work matters and asked if I could get you settled in." He pushed his glasses up his nose and smiled. "Are you ready for a night of demon hunting?"

"I'm hoping I don't find one," I said. "Demons never play nice when they're being hunted."

Gregor rubbed the back of his neck and frowned. "It's a bad business going on here. I'm concerned about Lex."

"You believe there really is a demon after him?"

"There's something, and not a pleasant something." He gestured us to follow him. "Where would you like to set up?"

"I'm planning to move around the castle during the night," I said. "We can start down here in one of the main rooms, but I'd like to go to Lex's bedroom at some point in the night. Do you think he'll have any objections?"

"He's willing to try anything," Gregor said. "This is plaguing him, but he's determined to make this castle his home."

We followed him into the living room. A warm amber glow from the overhead chandelier filled the room with light. It felt like the least likely place to house a demon, but I had to start somewhere.

"Will this be a suitable place to do your magic?" he asked.

"It looks good to me," I said. "I'm going to try some reveal spells. That will encourage anything with powers to come out."

"Whatever it is, I hope you can fix it, or banish it, or whatever needs doing." Gregor looked around the room. "I tell you, if I wasn't such a geek when it came to history, I wouldn't have taken this job. Lex warned me this was an unusual property, but some of the things I've seen, they could make your hair stand on end."

I set my bag and the food on the table. "Like what?"

"Objects moving, cold spots, things disappearing. The work crew is always complaining about tools vanishing and turning up in random rooms, rooms we've barely started work on."

"The ghosts are playing with you," I said. "I wouldn't worry if that's all they do. I've met a castle ghost. She didn't like me."

"It's taken me a while to get used to them, but in the time I've been here, not one has harmed me. I've never felt under threat by the ghosts."

"What about this demon, though? Lex is convinced something evil is here."

"I've seen nothing to support that theory," he said. "But I see no reason why he'd lie. And he's convinced this demon will influence him to do something bad. I've been literally chaining him to the bed, so he doesn't hurt himself. I've done plenty of weird things for previous clients, but this tops it."

I laid out my herbs and spell book as I looked around the room. "Was there anything on this site before the castle was built?"

His green eyes sparkled. "I thought the exact same thing. Maybe this dark presence is connected to an ancient spirit connected to the land or an older building."

"What did you discover?" I asked.

"This is the first and only building that has ever been on this land. It wasn't used for anything until the castle was put up."

"What about an ancient burial ground or sacrificial site?"

Gregor rubbed the tops of his arms. "No. Nothing like that came up in my research. I hope whatever you find, it's easy to get rid of. The jumpier Lex gets, the worse I get. I've never been good with my nerves, and I'd hate to let Lex down by not finishing this project."

"You're thinking of abandoning Lex before finishing the renovation?" I asked.

"I really hope it doesn't come to that," he said. "He's a great guy. I've worked with some terrible clients in my time. Sometimes, money and privilege can make a person entitled. They treat you like you're barely more than a slave, ordering you around and expecting you to work overtime. Lex is nothing like that. He's considerate and remembers that we all have lives outside our work."

"None of the team you're looking after have any problem with him?" I suggested. "Maybe this demon is just someone playing a cruel joke."

"It's not that. Lex is a decent employer. He's always going out and buying the crew meals and letting them leave early on the weekend. And the pay's generous too. I thought I'd landed on my feet when I got this gig. If the demon keeps causing problems for Lex, I worry he might snap. His state of mind seems fragile."

"Let's hope my investigation tonight sorts it all out," I said. "Then you can keep working here, and Lex can stop stressing out."

"Yes, let's hope so. The very best of luck with your mission." He turned to the door.

"Do you have a room in the castle?" I asked.

He shook his head and laughed softly. "You won't get me staying here overnight. I have a yurt in the grounds. It's not far from here. It's spacious and has everything I need. Plus, there are absolutely no ghosts or demons sliding in to cause me any problems."

That didn't leave me full of confidence. If Gregor wasn't prepared to sleep in the castle, it didn't bode well for what I was about to find during this investigation.

We said goodnight, and Gregor left Wiggles and me alone.

I was just getting settled on the couch and flicking through my spell book when Lex walked in. He was dressed in green silk pajamas with a black robe over the top.

"Tempest, I wanted to see you before I turned in for the night," he said. "My apologies for not greeting you sooner, but my work keeps me busy. Did Gregor give you everything you need?"

"We're all set," I said.

"Excellent." He looked around the room. "Sensing anything?"

"It's too soon to tell. Nothing bad yet."

"That sounds promising. Maybe you being here will scare away the demon."

I arched an eyebrow. "You think I'm that intimidating?"

"Oh! That came out wrong." Lex waved a hand in front of him. "My brain's so weary, I'm not thinking straight."

I chuckled. "I get it. No worries. I'll be here all night to keep an eye on things."

"I wish you the very best, and I'll leave you to it before I put my foot in it again," Lex said. "My room's upstairs, the third door on the right, if you need me. And I've asked Gregor not to chain me to the bed tonight, so if you wish to speak to me at any time, come find me."

"Good to know. I'm sure there won't be any problems. Try to get a good night's sleep. I'll stop by later and check your room's all clear. I'll do my best not to disturb you."

With a final goodnight, Lex left us to it.

"All this chaining to the bed business sounds a bit kinky to me," Wiggles said after Lex had left the room.

"It's unusual," I said. "And a determined demon would break through those chains. Lex is still vulnerable. If that demon really wants him gone, he'll be dead before the next full moon. It seems he's being toyed with."

"The demon's trying to make him lose his mind?" Wiggles asked.

"Gregor said Lex's mind is fragile. Maybe that's exactly what the demon planned all along, torment Lex and send him crazy. Then he'll do her job for her by jumping off the castle roof."

"Huh. All this murderous demon talk is making me hungry." He nudged the food bag. "How about we eat?"

"Excellent plan." I pulled out the food and had just taken the first bite of a delicious bacon and cheese sub when the overhead lights flickered.

"Do I sense a demon?" Wiggles whispered.

"Or faulty wiring."

I tensed as the room was consumed by darkness for a few seconds.

"Beware." A faint female voice drifted past my ear.

I kept on eating. "Of what?"

"Evilllllll."

"Sister, we're the most evil things in this castle," Wiggles said. "You're gonna have to do better than that to make us run."

"Don't encourage the ghost," I said.

"Leave this place," the ghost whispered.

"You're only jealous because you can't eat," Wiggles said. "I'll be the same when I'm dead. I'll miss pizza more than Tempest."

"Thanks a lot," I said. "Although, I get what you're saying. Chocolate muffins probably taste different in the afterlife."

The ghost growled, and Wiggles growled back twice as loudly.

I grinned. "That was much scarier than the ghost. You win."

He huffed out smoke, a satisfied look on his face. "I always do."

There was a yell from an upstairs room.

"That didn't sound like a ghost." I jumped to my feet and raced to the door, Wiggles at my heels. "Where did it come from?"

"Tempest! Get up here!" Lex's pale face appeared at the top of the stairs.

"Is it the demon?" I raced up the stairs two at a time.

He nodded and grabbed my arm. "In the garden. This way." He pulled me to a window.

I stared out at a glowing figure about half a mile away. "That doesn't look like a demon."

"That's her! That's how she always appears to me," he said.

"Are you sure that's the demon who whispers to you?"

"Absolutely. She always glows like that."

The glow around the figure vanished, and everything outside went dark again.

"Do you think she's coming inside?" I asked. "Is this what she usually does?"

"She never comes inside this early," he said. "Something's wrong."

"Stay here. I'll take a look outside," I said.

"No! I want to come with you," Lex said. "I have to confront her. There must be an end to this."

My gaze ran over his silky pajamas. "At least put some boots on."

Color flooded his cheeks. "Of course. I'm panicked. Not thinking straight. Yes, boots. Good idea."

We dashed down the stairs, and I headed outside with Wiggles.

Lex joined us a few seconds later, wearing a pair of walking boots and a jacket over his pajamas. "It's this way. We need to go through the trees to find her."

I cast a ball of light over our heads as we hurried past the castle and into a small dense patch of trees.

"She was right around here," Lex said. "There's an abandoned cottage that used to be for grounds workers. I often see her out this way when I'm watching from the castle."

"I don't see any sign of a glow now," I said.

"It's right this way," Lex said. "You'll catch her, Tempest. You'll put a stop to this demon's meddling in my life."

I was panting by the time we reached the cottage. It was flint stone, missing a roof, and all the windows were broken.

"There's someone here!" Lex dashed ahead.

"Slow down," I yelled. "If it's the demon, you don't want to confront her head on." That never ended well, especially if you caught a demon unawares.

"It's not a demon," he yelled back. "I think it's a... person."

I glanced at Wiggles. "Who'd be out here this late?"

"Someone pretending to be a demon to make Lex go crazy," Wiggles said.

I rounded the corner of the cottage and pulled up sharply. Half the back wall had collapsed, and under a large pile of jagged flint was a person. Bare legs and dainty feet were visible. One delicate ballet pump had fallen from a foot, leaving it bare.

I raced forward and began removing the rocks. "Help me," I said to Lex, who stood there looking stunned.

"She's not the demon?" He lifted off a rock.

"Those legs don't look demon to me." I slowed as I uncovered a mass of pale hair.

Lex staggered back and dropped the rock he was holding. "No! It can't be."

"You know who this is?" I checked for a pulse. There was no sign of life, but she was warm. This had only just happened.

Lex dropped to his knees, a choked sob coming out of his mouth. "Can you see her face?"

I stroked away some of the hair, but the woman was face down. "Not really."

"Roll her over," he said.

"We shouldn't touch her too much."

"Please! I have to be sure."

"Of what?"

"I think... no, I'm imagining things." Agony strained his words. "Tempest, please. I have to see her face."

"Okay. But you're taking the blame if the angels get angry that we moved her." The second my hand touched her bare skin, pain lanced up my arm. I shook out my fingers.

"What's the matter?" Lex asked.

"She's pinned by magic," I said. "Someone used a spell to hold her down."

He groaned. "I have to know who this is."

I glared at him. "You're acting like you already know her."

"It's that hair. It's so familiar, but it can't possibly be her." His shoulders sagged, and he closed his eyes.

I shook my head and sighed. "Give me a minute to get rid of this magic." I ran through a magic eraser spell several times.

The magic that held the woman felt old, and it didn't want to budge. But as I continued to shove my magic into the woman's body, the spell faded enough so I could move her without getting a painful shock.

I gently caught hold of her shoulder and rolled her onto her back. "So, do you know who this is?"

Lex groaned again and dropped his head into his hands. "That's my wife."

# Chapter 6

My gaze flicked from Lex to the body. "How is that possible? I thought you were a widower?"

He gasped out air, his body shaking as he lowered his hands and stared at the woman on the ground. "I don't... I mean, how is this..." His words trailed off as his face drained of color, and he swayed from side to side.

I caught his shoulder and eased him all the way to the ground. "Take some deep breaths." If I wasn't careful, he'd pass out, and I'd have two bodies to deal with.

"Is she really..." Lex cleared his throat. "Are you sure she's dead?" He swiped at his eyes.

"Almost certain," I said. "But I'll double check in case I missed something." I turned to the body and examined her, but there were no signs of life. I wasn't sure what had killed her, the magic that held her to the ground or the wall falling on top of her. Maybe it was a combination of both. The magic could have trapped her in place, so she was unable to move while the wall was smashed over by her killer.

I walked back to Lex. He was still gasping in air and looking shaky. "How is she?"

"Still dead. We can't do anything to save her."

"We can bring her back!"

My eyebrows shot up, and I shook my head. "You want to reanimate your dead wife?"

He grabbed my leg and clung to it, desperation in his red-rimmed eyes. "That's possible. And if she's only recently died, it's much easier."

"I wouldn't say easy." I glanced at Wiggles and pressed my lips together. "It's intense magic, and only effective about ten percent of the time. If you attempt it on your wife, she might come back, but she'll not be anything like the woman you married. Trust me. I've got experience with this."

"You've reanimated a person?" His fingers scrabbled on my leg. "Then you must do that to my wife."

"No, not a person."

"Tempest and Aurora reanimated me." Wiggles strutted around looking pleased with himself. "Don't I look good? Some jerk ran me over. Tempest and her sister brought me back to life. As you can see, I'm a new and improved version of the average dog I used to be."

"What Wiggles is trying to tell you is that he came back but as a hellhound. If we were to try this magic on your wife, you might get more than you bargained for. Plus, attempting it on a person is so much more complicated than an animal."

"I'm confused." Lex slumped back onto the ground and covered his eyes with his hands. "She can't be here. How is she here?"

That's what I wanted to know, especially since I was certain Aurora told me Lex was widowed.

I looked up as footsteps approached. Gregor appeared, wearing jogging bottoms and a gray T-shirt. "I heard shouting. Is everything okay?"

"Everything's far from okay." I walked over to him. "We've found somebody in the grounds. She's not alive."

He took a step back, and his eyes widened. "What happened?"

I looked over at Lex, but he was in no condition to speak as he muttered under his breath and kept wiping away tears.

"We spotted someone from the castle. Lex thought it was the demon. He gave chase, and I followed. What we discovered was a woman crushed under a brick wall."

"Not just a woman," Lex muttered, "my dead wife."

Confusion crossed Gregor's face. "I don't understand. I thought your wife died in a landslide."

"Well, if she did, she's come back to life and returned here," I said. "Have you seen a woman hanging around the castle?"

Gregor scrubbed his chin. "People come to the castle most days to see what we're doing. I've spoken to several women about the work."

"Come take a look at the body," I said. "Perhaps you can identify her. I don't know her. She doesn't live in Willow Tree Falls."

"It's Florentine," Lex said. "I know my wife when I see her."

I raised my eyebrows at Gregor. Lex might be in shock and was seeing things that weren't there. "I'd appreciate the help."

"Oh, well, of course." The reluctance was clear on Gregor's face as he walked slowly toward me.

"Don't worry. It's not gory."

"I'm glad to hear it. Although, I imagine looking at any dead body isn't going to be particularly pleasant."

I shrugged. "Fair point."

Gregor patted Lex on the shoulder, pausing for a few seconds. "I'm so sorry. What a terrible thing to happen."

"I don't understand it," Lex said. "Florentine is dead. I buried her two years ago."

Gregor's gaze shifted to me, and he gave a discreet shrug before patting Lex's shoulder again. "We'll figure this out. Don't you worry." He walked the short distance to the fallen wall and stood beside me.

"We had to move her, so Lex could see her face," I said. "He recognized the hair. That's when he fell apart. He's convinced it's his wife. What do you reckon?"

Gregor's jaw was slack as he stared at the woman, and he shuddered.

I nudged him with my elbow. "You know her?"

His mouth moved, but no words came out.

I caught hold of his shoulders and turned him to face me. "I know it's a shock seeing a dead person, but I could do with a hand here. Who is she?"

He blinked rapidly before he turned to stare at the woman again. "I, well, I didn't know she was Lex's wife."

"You must have seen pictures of her in the castle."

He shook his head. "No, Lex doesn't like to have them out. He told me they make him sad. This really is his wife?"

"That's what he says, but he could be mistaken." I lowered my voice. "Maybe she just looks like his wife, and the shock of finding her made him imagine things. I want him to take another look, but it might push him over the edge."

Gregor scrubbed a hand across his eyes and took a step back. "I don't know who she is."

My gaze narrowed as he took another step away. "You're sure acting like you know her."

His anxious gaze flickered around. "No. This can't be right. She can't be his wife."

"But she is," Lex said softly.

Gregor looked at the body again and licked his lips. "We should get help."

I certainly needed help with these two out of action and looking shell-shocked. "Go to Angel Force. They need to know about this. Do you know where their building is? Someone will be on duty."

Gregor stumbled back before nodding. "Yes! Good idea. I'll go get them now." He looked at the woman one more time before turning and racing away through the trees, quickly disappearing from view.

I returned to Lex's side and sat next to him on the ground. "Tell me what happened to your wife. I mean, the first time she died. Was there any way there could have been a mistake in her identification? The woman who died wasn't Florentine?"

He shook his head and cleared his throat before running his hands through his hair several times. "No, no mistake."

"Are you up to talking about what happened to her? Was her death from natural causes?"

He blew out a long breath. "It was. My wife was an explorer. She loved to visit new places and hunt for hidden treasures. It's part of our nature. As jinn descendants, we enjoy uncovering forgotten hordes of treasure and claiming them."

"She died doing that?"

Lex nodded as his gaze went to the body. He looked away and shuddered. "She was exploring a site rumored to have ancient Mexican artifacts. They were supposed to be hidden high up on a mountain. She'd been searching for weeks and believed she was close."

"You didn't go with your wife when she looked for these treasures?"

"She didn't want me to. That's the tricky thing being married to another jinn. We'd have claimed the treasure for ourselves. That can lead to problems in a marriage."

"You don't share?"

A hard smile crossed his face. "Jinn aren't known for willingly sharing their treasure."

"When did you last have contact with her?"

"The day she died." He looked at the body. "The first time she died, I mean. She was so excited about what she was about to find. Florentine loved her treasure. Anyway, that was the last I heard from her. She died in a landslide. The mountain was unstable. People weren't supposed to be walking up it, which was part of the reason the treasure hadn't been discovered."

"And you actually saw her body after the landslide?"

"I saw it, and I collected it. I buried her in her hometown as she requested." A sob broke from his lips. "I'm sorry. As you can imagine, this is a terrible shock."

"And there's absolutely no way you identified the wrong person?" I asked. "I don't mean to make you sound stupid, but if she'd been badly injured, perhaps her face was hard to identify."

"No, it was her. And yes, she did have head injuries, but I'd know my wife anywhere." He raised a shaking hand. "And that's her."

I looked at Wiggles, who sat in front of us, listening to the conversation with interest. I shrugged at him, at a loss what to say. Someone had made a mistake. Either Lex had gotten things wrong the first time his wife died, or he'd misidentified this person. A person couldn't die twice.

"What makes you so sure this is your wife?" I asked.

He glanced at me, a glimmer of anger in his eyes. "Because I know my own wife."

"I've not seen any photographs of her in the castle. She could just look uncannily like her. You haven't seen her for two years. Memory can play tricks on you."

He sighed. "Not mine. And you won't see any pictures. It's too painful to see them every day and remember what I've lost. My relocation to Willow Tree Falls was supposed to help me move on. People were telling me I was living in the past, and I had to find a new challenge to tackle."

"So, you bought a ruined, haunted castle thinking it would help you?"

"Why not? I love old buildings, and when I saw this castle, it called to me. Just like me, it's suffered loss and has been damaged over the years. I wanted to restore us both and bring life back to this castle. I've felt like something's missing ever since I buried Florentine."

"But you can't have buried her," I said, "not if she's here."

He shrugged, a look of abject helplessness on his face.

"What was she doing hiding in your grounds? If she'd discovered where you'd moved, surely she'd want to see you."

Lex started several sentences but never got past the first few words. "I don't know." His hand went to his chest. "When she died, the pain was unimaginable. I thought I was over that, but it feels like it's starting again. She's dead, but she's here. She was alive, and now she's dead again? I don't understand. All I know for certain is that Florentine died two years ago. I buried her with her family by my side. We grieved for her. Was she really not dead all this time?"

I stared through the trees for a moment, giving Lex time with his shock and grief as I figured out how to ask the next question. Lex had been seeing a demon around the castle. A female had been haunting his dreams, telling him to do dark things. Could the demon and his dead wife be one and the same?

I sucked in a breath. I had to ask, even though he might hate me for it.

"There's dark magic at work here," he said before I'd had a chance to speak. "That's the only explanation."

Perhaps this wouldn't be as difficult as I'd thought. "I was wondering the same thing. Could it be more than a coincidence that you were pestered by this female demon, and now your wife's body appears?"

His head shot up, and he stared at me with wide, terrified eyes. "Could she be demon possessed?"

My mouth twisted to the side. "Demon possession only lasts as long as the host's alive. We got here not long after this woman died. That leaves two options; the demon would have perished, or it found a new host."

He blinked at me several times. "I... I don't understand."

"If your wife had been possessed by a demon, the demon would have had only a few moments to find a new host. When a demon joins with another individual, that's it. They're in for life."

"Don't you eat demons?" he asked. "Are you telling me you're full of demons bound to you?"

"Just the one," I said. "But I do have the ability to house demons inside me temporarily. I can only have one bound to me. The same rules would apply to your wife. Is it possible she was reanimated, and a demon took possession of her body the first time she died?"

He smacked the palm of his hand against his head. "I don't know. Can you see if she has demon marks on her?"

I stood and looked at the body. "They don't usually mark their host. You can tell someone's demon possessed by their behavior, and their... smell." That was a talent unique to Crypt witches. We could sometimes sniff out demons.

"Please, check. We must be sure. It would explain why she's here. Some foul demon took possession of her beautiful body and has been using it. My poor Florentine."

I thought about trying to explain demon possession to Lex again, but in his shocked state, he wasn't processing new information well.

"I'll take a look." I went back to the body and carefully brushed the hair away from her face. She looked unmarked other than a few cuts from where the rocks must have struck. The angels would kill me if they saw me messing with the body, but I did a quick check of any parts that were exposed. Everything looked normal.

I pressed my hand to her unmoving chest and closed my eyes. There was nothing there. If a demon had been inside her, it died when she did.

I removed my hand and turned slowly to stare at Lex, my pulse kicking up a gear. Or perhaps it hadn't perished. It found a new host and was lurking inside of Lex, keeping a low profile.

"Anything?" he asked as I returned slowly to him.

"No. Your wife's body no longer houses a demon, if it ever did."

"That must be the explanation," he said. "It's the only thing that makes sense. Not that much of this makes any sense."

I lowered a few barriers and allowed Frank's energy to trickle up my spine. He was always good at spotting other demon friends lurking around. He'd know if Lex was demon possessed and if it had jumped from his wife's body into his.

And Lex had been first on the scene. In his shock, he'd have no idea what was going on if the demon had leap-frogged into him.

Frank grumbled inside my head. "What are we doing?"

"Lex, do you mind if I run a couple of tests on you?" I asked.

His eyebrows lowered, his gaze running over me. "What kind of tests? To find what?"

"What do you think, Frank?" I talked to him inside my head, not wanting Lex to know what I had planned. If there was a demon inside him, it would make its move quickly when it realized it had been discovered.

"I think I'm bored," Frank said.

"Do you sense any demons?"

He growled in my head. "You want me to do your job for you?"

"Tempest," Lex said. "What's going on?"

I dropped another barrier. Frank's energy tingled down my arm, making me warm, and sweat bloomed across my forehead.

Lex shuffled back, using his hands to pull himself away. "Your eyes are glowing. What are you doing?"

I had enough of Frank's energy flowing through me to know I could take down a minor demon without too much trouble. "Stay right where you are. This might tickle." I dropped to my knees and placed my hands on either side of Lex's head.

He gasped and struggled in my grip, but I held on tight.

"Tempest! Explain yourself."

I grinned, Frank's dark amusement filtering through me at the sight of the startled jinn.

"How entertaining. Your new employer is entangled with demons," Frank said.

I shook my head. "I don't sense any, other than you."

Lex squirmed in my grip. "Who are you talking to?"

My hands tightened on his head, trying to find any sign of a demon inside him. "Stay still."

My voice had dropped an octave as Frank's energy pounded through me.

Lex did as I'd ordered, finally sensing how much danger he was in if I lost control of Frank.

I lowered a hand and shoved it inside his pajama top. Other than his racing heart, there was nothing there. He wasn't demon possessed.

I dropped my hands, stood and stepped away, shaking out the tingling feeling in my arms as I slowly placed the barriers back in position. "Thanks, Frank."

He grumbled. "You owe me."

"That's what you always say." I sucked in a deep breath as the heat faded inside me and focused on Lex. "If there was a demon inside your wife, it's no longer alive. I thought it might have crawled inside you in your panicked state. I had to be sure you weren't in danger."

"Oh!" Lex patted his arms and chest. "I don't feel any different. Am I safe?"

"I can confirm you're completely demon free."

He crawled toward me on his hands and knees and grabbed my leg. "Please, help me figure this out. You're the only one I trust. You understand demons."

I eased his fingers off my leg. "I'm not sure how I can help."

"You must find out what happened to my wife. How can she have been alive all this time? Was her first death a lie? What happened here? Was she too scared to come see me? And how did she die? Was this an accident? Did someone murder my wife?"

"That's a lot of questions and ones I have no idea how to answer," I said.

"I have to know," he said. "I'll give you anything you want. Name it and it's yours. I'm at your disposal. I thought the demon hunting me would send me crazy, but this is another level of insanity. I won't be able to rest until I know how my dead wife came to be here and what happened tonight."

The sound of beating wings had my head snapping up. Two angels swept down from the sky.

Dazielle and Cassiel landed neatly before folding their wings behind their broad shoulders and striding toward us.

Dazielle's bright blue gaze ran over me, and she scowled. "What a surprise. You're at a murder scene."

"I'm not sure it is a murder," I said.

She waved a hand in the air. "Whatever it is, you need to leave."

"No!" Lex pulled himself to his feet and brushed down his dirty pajama knees. "Tempest is staying right here."

Dazielle sighed. "Mr. Fontaine, I understand from your employee, Gregor, that you've had a shock tonight. You don't know what you're saying. Tempest—"

"Is staying," he said. "She's helped me, and she'll continue to do so."

"But we're here now. We can handle things," Dazielle said. "Tempest isn't an expert."

"I disagree." Lex pulled back his shoulders and nodded at me. "Which is why I'm hiring her as my consultant. I want her to work on this case alongside you to find out exactly what happened to my wife."

I locked gazes with Dazielle as she glowered at me. This was going to be fun.

# Chapter 7

If Dazielle's eyebrows rose any higher, they'd join her hairline.

I'd just finished explaining the situation in front of us, outlining who Lex thought the dead woman was.

Her lips pursed, and she folded her arms over her chest. "This is unusual. Mr. Fontaine, you are certain this is your wife?"

"I've already asked him that," I said. "He looked twice. This is Florentine Fontaine."

"I, this is... I don't feel good." Lex's jaw wobbled, along with his knees. He was too shocked to form a complete sentence anymore.

Dazielle tugged on the end of her long blonde plait before nodding at Cassiel. "Do a preliminary examination of the body. Check for any... abnormalities."

"And she's not a demon or possessed by one." I followed after Cassiel. "I already checked."

She turned and planted her hand against my chest, pushing me back less than gently.

I grunted but continued to chase her. "That's why I'm here. Lex believes he's the subject of a demon's attention."

I looked over at Lex, but he seemed lost in his own thoughts and wasn't backing me up.

"Run that by me again." Dazielle joined Cassiel by the body. "This is the work of a demon?"

"It might be." I lifted my hands. "I was here tonight looking for evidence of any demons in the castle. Lex has been pestered by a malevolent presence for months. It's gotten worse since he moved to Willow Tree Falls. He spotted something in the grounds, and we gave chase. That's when we discovered the body."

"She's definitely dead." Cassiel stood from her brief examination.

"Top marks go to you," I said. "We must have missed the wall falling on her by minutes."

"How can you be sure of that?" Dazielle asked.

"Because, unfortunately, I've been around enough bodies to know when somebody has just died," I said. "And magic was involved."

"Is that correct?" Dazielle asked Cassiel.

She gave a curt nod. "There's magic here. It's fading, though. Some sort of restraining spell or immobility spell was used on the victim."

"Something that trapped her, so she wouldn't have been able to move when the wall fell," I said.

"Did you see that happen?" Dazielle asked.

"No, we were too late."

"And I sense no demons around here," Dazielle said.

"Other than Tempest's low-level emissions," Cassiel said.

"What are you talking about? I'm emitting nothing."

"You always have the tang of something demonic about you." Cassiel's top lip curled.

"Cassiel's particularly sensitive to demons," Dazielle said. "You always give her a headache when you're around."

"There's nothing I can do about that," I said. "Frank's here to stay."

"Lucky us," Dazielle said. "What can you tell me about this body, Cassiel?"

"This was a recent death, less than an hour ago. There are several blows to the head that could have killed her. There's also a diminishing amount of magic involved."

"Is there anything odd about her that suggests she wasn't alive?" I asked.

"Meaning?" Cassiel frowned at me.

"If this is Lex's wife, she's supposed to have died two years ago. She shouldn't be here."

"This woman was one hundred percent alive before being, well, dead again," Cassiel said. "How that happened, I cannot explain."

Lex groaned, and his head sank into his hands again.

"There must have been a mistake the first time Florentine was declared dead." I kept my voice low, so Lex wouldn't overhear. "She died while exploring a mountain in Mexico. Landslide, apparently. Lex identified the body, and she was buried. But maybe he identified the wrong person."

"That sounds unlikely," Dazielle said.

"What's your explanation? You can't die twice," I said.

"We'll need further tests and examinations. Cassiel, arrange to have the body returned to Angel Force and make this job a priority. We'll close down this scene and check for evidence."

"Which means I need to leave?" I said.

"Correct," Dazielle said. "Mr. Fontaine may have utilized your services to investigate this death, but that doesn't mean we're working together."

"But we're not working against each other," I said.

"And if you find anything useful, you're to pass it on to me," Dazielle said.

I huffed out a breath. She always tried my last nerve. "And if you do the same for me, we can solve this thing twice as quickly."

"I'll consider it." She lifted her chin and glanced at Lex. "Get him out of here and keep an eye on him."

"You think he's involved?"

"It's nearly always the husband who kills their other half. Listen to see if he makes any mistakes. He could be hiding something."

"It can't be him," I said. "I was thirty seconds behind Lex."

"He was the one who alerted you to seeing the glowing figure in the grounds. Maybe he set this all up. You're supposed to be his alibi."

I hadn't thought of that. Had this simply been one big set-up? The hauntings? The demon? "We'll go back to the castle."

"I'll be there shortly." Dazielle turned her back on me and spoke to Cassiel. I'd been dismissed.

"Let's go, Wiggles." I walked over to Lex and helped him to his feet. "There's nothing we can do here. The angels will start the investigation into what happened. Let's get inside."

He nodded as he trudged along beside me. I caught hold of his elbow, not liking how pale he looked. If he fainted on me, there was no way I'd be able to carry him back to the castle.

"I'm so confused," he muttered. "Is this a nightmare? Has the demon finally taken possession of my mind?"

"Sorry to say, this is all real. I'm here, your wife's back there, and we need to figure out what happened."

He moaned softly. "Two years Florentine has been alive, and she never told me. She didn't reach out and make contact. Why?"

"Where were you in the castle when you saw the glowing figure?" I asked. "I'm assuming that figure was Florentine."

"No! Although, I don't know anymore. It was the same spot I saw the glow. I was in my room when I saw it. Ever since the problems with the demon have intensified, my sleep's been fragmented. I try to keep awake as late as possible, so I don't have to endure the constant whisperings and suggestions to do myself harm. I was sitting by the window and reading when the glow caught my eye."

"You were alone in your room?" That wasn't a great alibi. True enough, I was in the castle, as was Wiggles, but Lex knew the layout of the castle better than I did. There must be several ways to get outside. He could have snuck down the stairs and out another door without me being aware of what he was doing. That would have given him time to kill this woman and easily make it back.

He scraped a hand down his face. "I called you after staring at the glow for several minutes. I thought it might be an illusion at first. Did this demon get her revenge by killing Florentine? Was Florentine coming to find me and the demon took away my chance of happiness?"

We reached the entrance to the castle, and I pushed open the door, waiting for Lex to trudge through, his shoulders slumped and his head down.

"Don't pin your hopes on this being demon related. I didn't get much chance to investigate, but I found no evidence of a demon within the castle," I said.

"She must have been here," he said. "And she finally found a way to break me. My Florentine was coming back, and the demon killed her."

I wasn't so sure about that. When demons killed, they liked to be messy. They left a statement, clear evidence they were more powerful than anyone else.

"I'll get us some coffee," I said once I'd settled Lex on the couch.

"Martha's available at all hours," he said. "Simply pull the cord in the hall. She'll get you anything you need."

My nose wrinkled. There was no way I was waking Martha just for a hot drink. "I'll be right back." I tilted my head at Wiggles, and he followed me.

I'd just left the living room, when Gregor appeared through the front door. "I got back as quickly as I could. What's happening? How's Lex?"

"Not good," I said. "Why don't you sit with him? I'm getting coffee for everyone, then we need to figure this out."

He licked his lips. "Do you think he'll want company?"

"It's best if we don't leave him on his own right now." Gregor was still being weird. I got that seeing a body was never on anyone's top ten list of fun things to do at midnight, but he looked guilty about something. Was he involved in this?

Gregor nodded. "Of course. This is a shock for him too." He hurried into the living room.

"He's an odd one," Wiggles said. "Elves are so sensitive."

"This whole situation is odd," I said. "What do you make of Lex?"

"He's a hot mess," Wiggles said. "He's whiter than some of the ghosts prowling around this castle."

"His shock appears genuine. Either that or he's an amazing actor."

"No surprise really that he's wigged out," Wiggles said. "The dead wife comes back to life, stalks you, and then dies again. Anyone's head would be a little screwed up after that."

"I can't figure it out." I walked along the hallway, checking in rooms to try to find the kitchen. I'd lost track of where everything was, given the size of the place.

"A demon and a dead wife who's not dead," Wiggles said. "That's one heck of a mystery."

"Here we are." I flicked on the lights and entered the large oak kitchen. I switched on the kettle and hunted around for mugs.

"Check for cookies too," Wiggles said. "Sugar's always good for shock."

"You're not in shock," I said.

"I am! I just saw a dead body."

"You hunt for the cookies. I'll make the drinks." I leaned against the marble worktop and crossed my arms over my chest. Something weird was going on, and I'd been dumped right in the middle of it. I wasn't sure I wanted to be.

I hadn't officially agreed to be Lex's consultant in this murder, if it even was a murder. It might be easiest if I backed out now before I got too involved.

I rubbed my forehead. Aurora would hate me. She'd find out what had gone on and insist I help. If I didn't, she'd accuse me of scuppering her chance of romance with Lex.

Mind you, would she want a romance with this guy, since he'd been technically married until about an hour ago, when his wife died again? That might put her off. Although, knowing Aurora, she'd see his good side, think he was the victim, and accuse me of being cold-hearted if I refused to help.

It looked like I had to stick this out, whether I wanted to or not.

Wiggles bounced out of the large walk-in pantry, three boxes of cookies jammed in his mouth.

"We don't need that many." I made the coffees and found a tray to set them on.

He spat the boxes on the ground. "We do. There are never enough cookies in the world."

I grabbed a cloth and wiped the dog drool off the packets of cookies before placing them on the tray and returning to the living room.

Lex hadn't moved from where I'd sat him, his fingers gripping the edge of the couch, and his eyes a little too wide to be healthy.

Gregor sat beside him, looking worried.

"Here, drink this." I passed Lex a strong coffee with several sugars in it, opened a box of cookies, and handed him one.

I sipped my own coffee, while Wiggles noisily munched several cookies.

Lex downed his coffee and shuddered. "Thank you, Tempest."

"What for?"

"Helping me. You didn't have to come here tonight and look for demons. You didn't have to follow me into the woods. And you could have said no when I told the angels you were my consultant."

I bit my lip. I wasn't doing this to help him. I was doing this because, if I didn't, my little sister would nag me to death. Still, Lex didn't need to know that. "Demons interest me. And I've worked with the angels before. I'm sure we can work on this together." So long as Dazielle didn't throttle me or have me arrested for getting in the way.

Gregor patted Lex's arm. "Do the angels have any idea what happened?"

"No more than we do," he said.

"The angels will want to know if you had problems with Florentine," I said. "Was your marriage happy?"

"Well, we had our moments." Lex glanced at Gregor. "We were happy in the beginning of our marriage."

"But things weren't so good toward the end?" I asked.

He sighed and shook his head. "Florentine could be obsessive about things."

"What sort of things did she obsess over?" I asked.

"The usual jinn interests."

"Treasure?"

"She loved anything bright and sparkly," Lex said. "The problem was, she'd never keep it. Her spending habit far exceeded the few trinkets she'd discover."

"Florentine had a problem with money?" I asked.

Lex lifted his head and his gaze went around the room. "It's so quiet and calm. Gregor, doesn't this space feel different to you?"

Irritation traced through me. Was Lex's grief all an act? "Getting back to your wife. Is there—"

"Wait a moment, Tempest." Lex stood and slowly turned, wonder in his eyes. "It's extraordinary. I didn't notice it when we first came in. I was so consumed with everything that's going on, but the castle feels light. It feels like a new home."

I looked at Gregor and frowned. "What does he mean?"

"I think I understand," he said. "The atmosphere has changed. I'm not sure if you noticed when you were here earlier, but there was always something about the castle that made me tense. It was as if someone or something was watching me. But now, there's nothing. Whatever was here has gone."

I pushed aside my annoyance and focused on the room. They were right. I'd sensed a low-level creepiness as soon as I'd entered. I'd simply assumed it was because the place was crammed full of ghosts, but even though a ghost had been flitting around in one corner of the room ever since we entered, it did feel peaceful. The atmosphere had shifted.

Lex's hand went to his mouth, and he sucked in a breath. "Could my wife have been behind these problems? Was she haunting me?"

"That's not possible," I said. "She's only just died, for the second time."

He scrubbed his chin. "Well, maybe a fake haunting? Was Florentine causing me all these issues? Now she's gone, and the place is transformed."

I tugged him back down to the couch. "Explain to me why you said things weren't great at the end of your marriage. What was the problem?"

He slumped forward, his elbows resting on his knees. "She was greedy and a liar. I also believe she was being unfaithful, but I had no proof. She was always discreet."

"Did she ever steal from you?" Wiggles asked.

"She would ask for money, which I gave her," he said. "I don't believe she would take something I had a claim on."

"She didn't ever get her hands on your jinn hoard?" Wiggles asked.

Lex gave a low, sad chuckle. "I have no hoard. Those days of acquiring massive amounts of gold, jewels, and treasures to keep for my own pleasure are no longer possible. I've had to move with the times and give up the dream of having a treasure trove at my disposal."

"This castle couldn't have been cheap," I said. "You must have some assets."

"It was a bargain," Lex said. "The previous owner was desperate to get rid of it. I'm rather embarrassed to say I paid a third of the market value. With the fire damage and its terrible reputation, it was easy to snap up. Even so, it cost a fair amount of money. Trust me, I didn't use my treasure hoard to pay for it, because I don't have one."

"Did Florentine have treasure you inherited when she died?" I asked.

"She had very little and was never content with what she had. I offered her a wonderful life with plenty of luxury, but it was never enough. It's part of our nature. We always desire more. It's one of the things I love about this castle. I knew it would take years to restore it to its glory, and I wouldn't get bored. Little did I know, I was also taking on a demon who'd push me to my limits. And now this." His head lowered, and his shoulders shook.

"Let's take a break," I said. "The angels will be here soon, and they'll want to question you."

"I'd appreciate some time alone," Lex said. "This evening has been a terrible shock. If you'll both excuse me, I need a few minutes." We all stood as Lex hurried out of the room.

Gregor caught hold of my elbow and stepped closer, clearing his throat as he did so. "I didn't want to say this in front of Lex, but there's something you need to know. It's about Florentine."

# Chapter 8

"What do you want to tell me?" I asked.

Gregor's jaw wobbled, and he swallowed.

I glanced at Wiggles, feeling vaguely horrified. Gregor was about to cry. "If you know what happened to Florentine, you need to tell me. Did you see Lex do something to her?"

"I didn't see who killed her." He pinched the bridge of his nose. "I was so shocked when I saw her there. I didn't know what to do."

"Of course, that's natural, especially now you know who she is."

He dropped onto the couch, and tears rolled down his cheeks.

I settled next to him and hovered my hand over his back before patting his shoulder. He must be upset on Lex's behalf, but he needed to man up and tell me what was going on.

Gregor swiped his hand across his face and sucked in a deep breath. "I knew her."

"You'd met Florentine before she died?"

"I didn't know her name was Florentine." His words came out shaky. "I knew her as Fay."

My brows lowered as more of Gregor's tears fell. "She was using a different name when you met her?"

"I had no idea she was Lex's wife. As you can see by looking around this room, he has no pictures of her anywhere. I didn't know that the woman who approached me was hiding her true identity."

"She approached you?" I asked. "When did you first meet?"

"The day I got the renovation job on the castle," he said. "I was in a great mood and had gone to dinner to celebrate getting this job. The restaurant was crowded, and Fay, or rather, Florentine, approached me and asked if she could sit at the spare seat."

"And you said yes?"

"She was a beautiful woman. I was more than happy to share my space with her. She spent the whole evening flirting and teasing me. It was like I'd found my perfect woman."

If Florentine knew that Lex had bought the castle, she'd most likely have known he was planning renovation work. She could have figured out who he'd employed to do it. Had she used Gregor to find out more about Lex's movements?

"What happened after you had dinner together?" I asked.

"She asked me out. We started seeing each other several times a week. I would have seen her every day if I could, but her work kept her busy, and she often had to travel."

"You were serious about her?"

He sighed. "Very much."

"Did you love her?" I asked him.

Gregor hung his head. "She was everything I'd ever wanted in a woman. She was beautiful, smart, and funny. And she was so interested in the castle and my work on the building. She'd ask me questions about the progress of the renovation every time we met. It was flattering that someone so beautiful took notice. Most women find the work I do tedious but not Fay."

"Why do you think she was so interested?" I asked. "Did she ever mention Lex?"

His tear-filled eyes lifted to mine. "I've been thinking about that ever since I learned who she was. Has she been using me? She wasn't interested in me at all..." His words broke, and he took a few seconds to compose himself. "Fay has made a fool of me. She didn't care. She wanted to know about her husband. This was never about us."

I patted his shoulder again. "It's a big possibility. Lex buys the castle, employs you, and Florentine just happens to turn up. Did she ever get inside the castle and look around?"

His eyes widened, and he swallowed. "Yes! Only once. She kept asking to look around, but I wanted to show it to her when it was finished. One night, when Lex was away, I snuck her in. She looked about for at least an hour and asked dozens of questions."

"About anything in particular?"

"Mainly about structural changes and if I'd found anything behind the walls. She told me she loved all the mystery that came with places like this. I had no reason to think she was lying. At least, I didn't."

"She was looking for something specific?"

He shrugged. "She must have been. What does this mean? What did she want?"

"Do you think she was in the grounds last night to see you or to watch Lex?"

Gregor removed his glasses and scrubbed at his eyes. "I wish I could say for certain she was here for me. She knew I stayed in the grounds when I wasn't working. I'd even shown her around my yurt." He groaned and dropped his head into his hands. "If Lex finds out I've been dating his wife, he'll fire me. I love this job. I can't lose it."

"Let's not worry about that just now," I said. "And, technically, you weren't doing anything wrong. Florentine deceived you. She used a false name when she met you. She was the one who approached you and turned on the charm. It's not like you went after her, knowing she was married to Lex. And besides, everyone thought she was dead."

Gregor blew out a breath and nodded. "I've gotten to know Lex since I've worked with him. I consider him a friend as well as an employer. This will hurt him. He must be in such shock over discovering that Fay, I mean Florentine, was alive. And it appears she knew exactly where he was. Why didn't she reach out to him?"

Despite Gregor's assurance that he had no idea who Florentine really was, he'd just provided an excellent motive for both him and Lex wanting her dead. Either of them could have learned what she was doing and decided to seek revenge.

Perhaps Lex saw Florentine with Gregor and realized she'd faked her death and was cheating on him. Or Gregor might have stumbled over a photograph of Florentine and put everything together. He'd figured out she'd been deceiving him to get information about the castle. She didn't love him. She was using him.

"Should I tell Lex what's happened?" Gregor asked.

"Let's not bother him for now," I said. "But the angels will need to know. This could be important in figuring out what Florentine was up to."

"They'll think I'm a suspect, won't they?" he said on a heavy sigh.

"They'll be interested in you." Just as I was. "If it's any consolation, can you even be charged with murder if the person you're supposed to have killed has already been declared dead?" Florentine was supposed to be dead. You can't kill a dead person.

"Oh! I didn't think about that." He scrubbed a hand across his chin. "It doesn't make me feel any better. This is confusing. I genuinely didn't know who she was."

"Take a step back. We have to figure out if this is really Florentine. If it is, we need to work out what happened the first time she was supposed to have died," I said. "We have to start from there."

"Of course." He sighed. "I promise you I'm not the sort of man who chases after somebody else's wife. I really thought she was the one. She was so sweet. Was it all a lie?"

"I can't answer that," I said. "Maybe Florentine really did care for you." Although, it seemed increasingly unlikely to me. The more I discovered about Florentine Fontaine, the less I liked her.

I turned and looked at the doorway as footsteps approached.

"I smell feathers," Wiggles muttered.

Dazielle strode in and nodded at us. Her gaze shifted to Gregor, and she tilted her head. "Is there a problem?"

"There might be," I said. "Have you found anything useful at the crime scene?"

Her eyes narrowed before she gave a quick nod. "There are no signs of a struggle. It appears the woman was crushed by the wall and incapacitated by the magic we discovered."

"It was dark magic?" I asked.

"No, but it felt like old magic," Dazielle said. "It dispersed quickly, so it was hard to get an exact fix on the type of magic, but it had an ancient quality to it."

"Like the kind of magic a jinn might use?" I asked.

Her wings fluttered around her before she nodded again. "Perhaps. What do you know about it?"

"I know nothing about the magic used on Florentine," I said. "But Gregor has something he needs to tell you."

He cleared his throat and stood before patting his chest. "I knew the dead woman. We were in a relationship."

I sat back and let Gregor tell Dazielle how he met Florentine. I felt a trickle of sympathy for him. He was clearly a guy obsessed with his work, and then some beautiful, flirty woman appeared in his life and wowed him. Gregor didn't stand a chance.

Florentine must have targeted him. She was using him, and it had something to do with the castle and Lex.

Gregor slumped back on the couch as if the effort of telling Dazielle his tale of woe had exhausted him. "I had nothing to do with her death."

"Where were you at the time of her murder?" Dazielle asked.

"Have you pinpointed the time of death?" I asked.

Her lips pressed together as she glared at me. "You were correct in your assumption that Florentine had only just died when you found her."

"I was in my yurt," Gregor said.

"Alone?" Dazielle asked.

"Of course. I was in bed when I heard Lex shouting. I came out to take a look and followed the noise."

"Where's your yurt?" Dazielle asked.

"I prefer to camp in the woods," he said. "I don't like to be too close to the castle; otherwise, the ghosts can be a nuisance. I had to move the yurt twice before I found somewhere they'd stay away from."

"Are you near the crime scene?" I asked.

He ducked his head. "A two-minute walk away."

"Let's go take a look around your yurt," Dazielle said.

He sighed and stood before giving a slow nod. "I understand this looks bad for me, but I didn't know who Florentine really was. I thought I'd finally got a lucky break when it came to finding love. I should have known it was too good to be true."

"Accidentally hooking up with your employer's dead wife is lousy luck," Wiggles said. "Best stay away from the hot women in the future. They always cause problems."

I suppressed a smile and tried to look sympathetic.

His head dipped. "I've learned my lesson. Stick to work. It's what I'm good at."

"Gregor, you were alone at the time Florentine was murdered. We need to discount you as a suspect," Dazielle said. From the glint in her blue eyes, that was the last thing she was thinking.

Gregor's worried gaze flicked to me. "Will Tempest be there?"

"She's a consultant on this case," Dazielle said, her tone making it clear how much she loathed that. "She may come with us but as an observer only."

I looked at Wiggles and winked. Dazielle was just hating this. I got a certain amount of satisfaction about being able to wind her up so easily.

This wasn't my fault. Lex had insisted I get involved. And for once, I'd actually get paid for doing this. Lex had promised me whatever I wanted.

We headed back outside, and Gregor led the way through the trees. It was a five-minute walk from the castle to his yurt, and Dazielle didn't acknowledge my presence the entire time.

That was fine by me. If she wanted to act like a brat because she was being forced to work with me, then I'd let her.

"Here we are," Gregor said. "This is home."

Far from the poky canvas tent I'd imagined, his yurt looked like a small circus tent with a circular frame and patterned red felt cover.

"How did you get this in through the trees?" I asked.

"It breaks apart," he said. "The walls expand on a lattice, and I use rods to erect the roof. It's made from an original Mongolian design. The frame's lashed together with rope."

"You have windows!" I was seriously impressed. I might even be tempted to camp if I had one of these.

"Wait until you see inside." Pride filled Gregor's voice as he untied the door flap.

Dazielle turned just before I entered and placed a hand on my shoulder. "Watch your step, Tempest. I know Lex wants you involved but don't go poking around where you're not wanted. I lead on everything here. I'll look around; you simply observe."

I winced as her fingers tightened on my shoulder. "You're the boss. Got it." At least, I'd let her think she was.

She grunted before turning and heading into the yurt.

I followed behind her and stood next to Gregor, happy to watch as Dazielle strode around and looked at the surprisingly spacious interior. There was a real bed, a small cabinet, a rack of clothes, a large desk, and a small area for cooking.

"It's a nice setup you've got in here," I said to him.

"I love it here. I can easily live in this all year round."

"It must get cold in the winter."

"No! It's insulated. And I can add layers to the structure to keep it warm," he said. "I often use it when I'm on a job. I'm not a fan of boxy caravans. They take too much effort to move. With this, I strap it to a vehicle and can bring it anywhere. It takes less than an hour to erect. All the furniture can easily be broken down, and I simply store it when I'm not using it."

"Tempest!"

I looked at Dazielle. "What's wrong?"

"Your hellhound is snuffling."

A laugh shot out before I could stop myself. "He's a hound. He likes to sniff."

"He's putting damp nose prints on everything." Dazielle shooed Wiggles away from the bed. "He could be destroying evidence."

"Take a swab of his nose. If any dog snot comes up on the evidence, you can discount it."

"I do not snot on things," Wiggles said.

"I'll make him wait outside if he keeps nosing about," Dazielle said.

Wiggles grunted. "I'd like to see you try."

Dazielle's eyes narrowed. "It's happened before." She moved to the table and spent a moment looking at the building plans laid out.

"Anything of interest?" I asked.

She shook her head. "Nothing useful."

A shaky sigh slid from Gregor's lips. "This is so tragic."

I grimaced. He was about to cry again. I wasn't great at dealing with the more sensitive side of murder. Maybe I should let Dazielle lead on this after all.

Gregor swiped his eyes. "Even though Fay hurt me, I still love her."

"How did she hurt you?" I asked.

His expression darkened. "She was so attractive. She drew a lot of attention."

"From other guys?" I asked. "Anyone in particular?"

"She ignored most of them. But there was someone she was interested in." He scowled and scrubbed a foot on the floor.

"Someone who might get angry if he figured out she was also seeing you?"

"Tempest!" Dazielle hissed.

I ignored her. "Go on. Who was she seeing?"

Gregor massaged his temples. "That hateful vampire from Unicorn's Trough."

# Chapter 9

My mouth dropped open. "Brogan Costin? Are you sure it was him?"

Dazielle strode over and nudged me with a wing, warning me I was treading on her toes, but I was so shocked Gregor had mentioned Brogan that I couldn't stop myself.

Gregor's nose wrinkled. "That's where I've seen him."

"Tall guy, tattoos, dark and sort of scary looking?" I asked.

A wing batted my arm and not in a friendly way.

He nodded. "That's him."

"Why do you think Brogan's involved in this?" Dazielle asked.

Gregor blew out a breath. "Fay was a wonderful woman. She was vivacious, kind and funny, and—"

"Yes, you've already mentioned her wonderful attributes," Dazielle said. "But why do you think she was also seeing Brogan?"

"I saw them together," he said. "They were being discreet, but I recognized her laugh. I was in the village getting supplies, and I heard her. I looked around but couldn't see Fay. Then I heard her laugh again. It was coming from a woman wearing a large hat, standing outside Unicorn's Trough. Her white hair was concealed under it; otherwise, she'd have been impossible to miss."

"What was she doing?" I asked.

"Meeting that vampire," Gregor hissed. "They hurried away from his café and headed toward the woods. I was so surprised to see her. She always met me in the evenings because her work kept her busy. I wondered if I'd made a mistake, but her laugh was so distinctive. I followed them, and when they got to the edge of the woods, they kissed."

"You're certain it was Florentine?" I asked.

I got a smack on the arm from Dazielle's wing for asking that question. "Quit hitting me! Your feathers hurt."

"Then stop asking the questions," Dazielle said.

Gregor's confused gaze flicked between us. "I was in no doubt. Her laugh was like gentle bells ringing in the breeze."

This guy had it so bad for Florentine. "Brogan and Florentine were dating at the same time you were seeing her?" I deliberately stepped aside to avoid Dazielle's wing strike.

"Yes! And the more I think about it, he must be involved with this. That vampire killed her." Gregor smacked a fist into his open palm. "He coerced her into dating him. She wouldn't like him. He's so... rough."

I scowled at him. Brogan wasn't rough, but they were different. Brogan was tall, broad, and covered in tattoos. Gregor rocked the geek chic look.

"How long did you follow them?" Dazielle asked.

"I was so upset when I saw them kiss that I stormed away," Gregor said. "I couldn't watch anymore."

"And you confronted Florentine?" I asked. "How did she take it?"

He rubbed the back of his neck as he shook his head. "I didn't. I was scared that, if I asked her to choose between us, she'd pick him."

"You were willing to share her with another guy?" I asked.

"You might think that's ridiculous, but I cared for her. And we'd never talked about being exclusive." He grimaced. "But the blame lies with the vampire. Fay would never be interested in him if he hadn't used his power on her. He was seducing her, and she could do nothing about it."

I glanced at Dazielle, who shrugged. Some vampires had the ability to coerce a person into doing something they didn't want to do, but it was hard and draining. Besides, Brogan was only a half-vampire. I wasn't even certain he had that ability. He was also a good-looking guy who attracted a lot of attention and was never short of admirers. He didn't need to use anything other than his charming smile to get women falling at his feet.

I bit my bottom lip as I remembered him saying he was off the market. Had he been referring to Florentine?

"What happens next?" Gregor asked. "Are you going to arrest the vampire?"

"We'll certainly speak to Mr. Costin," Dazielle said. "We need to talk to everyone who knew Florentine."

"He did this," Gregor said. "He has to be behind her death. He abused my sweet Fay, and when she realized what he was doing and fought back, he killed her."

"Why didn't he drain her blood?" I asked. "Why drop a wall on her head?"

Gregor went very pale. "To hide his involvement? That's for you to find out."

"And we will," Dazielle said, her angry gaze on me.

"May I ask one thing," Gregor said. "Please, don't tell Lex about my involvement unless you absolutely have to. This is a dream job, despite the ghosts. I'd hate to lose it because of this. I genuinely didn't know who Fay, or rather, Florentine, was."

"We'll be as discreet as possible," Dazielle said. "Get some rest. I'll send someone to see you tomorrow." She inclined her head toward the yurt flap, and I nodded goodbye to Gregor before heading out with Wiggles.

"What do you make of that?" Dazielle asked.

"I'm not sure about Brogan being involved." I kicked a stone along the ground as we walked away. "Gregor might have gotten desperate and pointed the finger at someone else to take the heat off him while he makes a run for it."

"You think it's a cover story?"

"I'm still trying to get my head around how a woman who's been dead for two years came back to life only to die again," I said.

Dazielle hummed under her breath. "It's a strange one."

I glanced at her. "What are you planning to do next?"

"Move the body back to Angel Force," Dazielle said. "Find out if this really is Florentine Fontaine before we do anything else. Although, no matter who she is, a woman died tonight in suspicious circumstances. This wasn't an accident."

"I agree," I said. "I'm heading home. I need to check on Cloven Hoof. Will I need to hassle you for updates on this case, or can we actually work together?"

She scowled at me. "I'll keep you informed." She picked up her pace and strode ahead, leaving me and Wiggles behind.

"Are we really going home?" Wiggles asked.

"Of course not," I said. "I want to speak to Brogan. Being a half-vampire means night is his time for having fun. We need to catch him before the angels start prodding him and see if he knows anything about Florentine."

"Or Fay," Wiggles said.

"Yeah, different names is not at all confusing," I said. "Did you pick up anything useful when you were sniffing around the yurt?"

"Nothing," he said. "I didn't smell the dead woman in there. It just smelt of ink, paper, and Gregor's broken heart."

"I sort of feel sorry for the guy. But he could be involved. He got jealous and struck out in fury."

"You think he knew Fay was really Florentine?"

"No. He was honestly shocked that the woman he was dating was Lex's wife. Although, maybe he's just a really good liar."

We walked along in silence for a moment.

"If we're going to Unicorn's Trough to find Brogan, we should check out the back alley behind his store first," Wiggles said.

"Why do we need to go back there?"

"Hunting for clues."

I smirked. "More like sniffing around in Brogan's trash to see if he's put spoiled food out."

"Food could have clues on it," Wiggles said. "You should never ignore any piece of pizza without giving it a thorough investigation with your tongue. You might miss something vital."

"The only thing I'll miss is food poisoning," I said. "You can check out the trash if you want. I need to speak to Brogan."

We hurried back to the village. It was already the early hours of the morning, and all the stores were shut. Even Cloven Hoof would be shutting in a few minutes.

We stopped outside Unicorn's Trough. I peered through the windows at the front. It was shut up, and the lights were off, but I knew that Brogan liked to take late night walks. He told me once that he felt more alive at night. Being a half-vampire, he could operate in the daytime, but night was when he really came alive.

"I'll go around the side," Wiggles said.

I arched an eyebrow at him. "Five minutes. If I have to come and pull you out of a trash can because you got stuck, I won't be happy."

"I'll be right back." He bounded into the shadows and along the alleyway.

I peered up at the apartment over the top of the café. Brogan lived in that apartment, but there were no signs of life. The windows were dark, and the curtains drawn.

I rubbed my arms as a chill breeze swept through the village. There was something creepy about skulking around in the dark hunting down a vampire.

Wiggles bounded out of the alley, two slices of pizza in his mouth and a muffin balanced on his head.

"You have got to be kidding me," I said. "You don't need that much food."

He swallowed one of the pizza slices. "The muffin's for you."

"I'll pass on your dumpster muffin. Come on. Let's walk around and see if we can find Brogan."

"Tracking vampires in the dead of night," Wiggles said. "This makes us seriously hard core."

"It's not just Brogan out here," I said. "He's got his scary granny and grandad staying with him. I bet they're out here somewhere. I still haven't forgotten how Granny Ana sniffed me like I was a piece of prime rib."

"She loved your stink," Wiggles said. "I wouldn't want to go up against her. I mean, I would if I had to. And I'd beat her. But she might get in a few nips before I took her out."

I slowed as we passed a hedgerow. A shuffling came from behind it.

"Vampire?" Wiggles whispered as he scoffed down the muffin.

I crept toward the hedgerow. There was something moving around behind the foliage.

Wiggles trotted to the other end of the hedge and poked his nose around the side.

"Eek!" He flew backward and rolled over, coming to a stop on his back.

I raced to his side. "What happened?"

Laughter came from behind the hedge before Bandit trotted out. "You should have seen the look on your furry face."

"Bandit! What are you doing out here?" I asked.

"I like the night time," she said as she chuckled at Wiggles. "Your rough, tough hellhound isn't up to much."

Wiggles scrambled to his feet and growled at her. "I wasn't scared."

"You so were. You squeaked like a startled mouse." Bandit curled her tail around her feet.

He bared his teeth and took a step toward her.

"Cool it, you two," I said. "We're supposed to be in silent mode. We'll wake the whole village if we keep on like this."

"What are you doing creeping around at night, anyway?" Bandit asked.

"I could ask you the same thing," I said. "Shouldn't you be keeping my sister company?"

"I only came out for a short while. Aurora complains if I need to use the bathroom in the middle of the night. She says it affects the smell of the whole store, and she has to cleanse it before the customers arrive. I decided to take a ten-minute break and stretch my legs. She's fine. Fast asleep with a smile on her face."

"Probably dreaming about Lex," I muttered.

"The posh guy from the castle? Why would she be dreaming about him?" Bandit asked.

"You don't need to know what's going on," Wiggles said. "We're dealing with this. This is our case. Isn't that right, Tempest?"

Bandit cocked her head. "What are you dealing with? Sounds interesting. Mind if I tag along?"

"I definitely do," Wiggles said. "You've got your own job now. Go back to Aurora."

She fluffed out her fur and hissed at him.

"Sorry, Bandit. It's probably best you're not here. And I don't like to think of Aurora being on her own for too long. She's been much happier since you moved in."

"That's because I make everyone's life better," she said. "But I can still hang out with you for a while, spread a little Bandit magic around. Grumpy Paws over there needs it."

"You can't hang out if you're not invited," Wiggles said.

I waved a hand at them, hoping they'd stop talking. "That's enough. We need to get moving."

"I'm coming with you." Bandit stood and followed along behind us.

"We'll just ignore you," Wiggles said. "You'll only get in the way."

"In the way of what?" Bandit said. "I can help. Remember when we went to that haunted castle, and I solved the murder?"

"You did no such thing." Wiggles snorted and kicked dust behind him.

I turned the corner and slammed straight into Brogan's chest.

I staggered back, and my gaze lifted to meet his. "Jeez! Don't do your creepy vampire thing on me."

He tipped back his head and laughed softly, flashing a hint of fang as he did so. "I couldn't resist. You and your troop of animals are noisy. I heard you from miles away. I believe you're looking for me?"

My eyebrows rose. "How do you know that?"

"You were at Unicorn's Trough a few minutes ago," he said. "I could smell you. I got curious and followed the noise."

"Oh, being sniffed out by a vampire isn't at all creepy," I said. Did I really smell so interesting to vampires? I might need to rethink my deodorant.

"No creepier than a demon carrying witch and a hellhound snooping around my café in the middle of the night," he said. "So, what gives?"

I glanced back at Bandit and Wiggles, who were engaged in a staring contest, before looking back at Brogan. "Do you know someone called Florentine Fontaine?"

He shook his head. "I've never heard of her, but the surname's the same as Lex's. Are they related?"

"They were married," I said. "She was his wife."

"I heard he was a widower. Did Florentine visit Willow Tree Falls before she died?"

"After that," I said.

Brogan's head drew back as his brows lowered. "I'm not sure I get your meaning."

"The late Mrs. Fontaine might not have been as dead as everyone thought," I said. "In fact, someone told me you were dating her."

A grin spread across his face. "I'm supposed to have dated a dead woman? What are we talking, a zombie? Demon possession of a corpse? No, a reanimated body?"

"Florentine didn't look anything like a zombie or a reanimated corpse when I discovered her body earlier this evening," I said.

"Oh!" His smile faded. "This isn't a joke. You found a body?"

I nodded. "And someone saw you with Florentine recently."

"What's this dead woman look like?"

"She's got long white hair and purple eyes."

Brogan's hand shot out to grab the tree next to him, holding himself up. "You mean Flossie?"

"Who's Flossie?" I asked.

"Flossie Burnett," he gasped. "She's my girlfriend. She's stunning, with long white hair that she hides under hats whenever she's out in public, sparkling purple eyes, and she has a laugh like a goddess."

I'd never heard Florentine laugh, but Gregor had also mentioned how appealing her laugh was. "That's not Flossie Burnett. That's Florentine Fontaine you're describing," I said. "Did she tell you her name was Flossie?"

Brogan sagged forward, his hands resting on his knee as he sucked in deep breaths. "This must be a mistake. I saw Flossie only two days ago. She had some business to deal with and said she wouldn't be around for a couple of days, but we'd arranged to meet tomorrow night."

"I'm not totally sure it's the same woman," I said. "I could be making a mistake, but you've just described the person I found tonight."

"How many white-haired, beautiful goddesses do you get in this place?" He shook his head. "Flossie's dead?"

I touched his arm. "Brogan, I think this woman's been lying to a lot of people. She was Lex's wife. Her real name was Florentine Fontaine. According to Lex, she died two years ago in a landslide. We haven't figured out how she did it yet, but until a few hours ago, she was very much alive."

"How did she die?" he whispered.

"That's something I'm also trying to figure out," I said. "Magic was used. We're looking at a homicide."

He groaned before pulling himself upright. Anger flashed across his face, and he snarled, exposing his fangs. "Who did this? You must have an idea."

It was never a good plan to anger a vampire. They were fast moving and deadly. Still, I needed to know the answers to my questions. "We're looking at anyone who had a connection to Florentine."

"Flossie! That was her name. That's how I knew her." Shock mingled with the anger in Brogan's eyes.

"Yes, and she also goes by the name of Fay," I said. "You weren't the only guy she was seeing while she was here."

He snarled again and took a step toward me. "Flossie was cheating on me?"

I stood my ground and glared up at him. "Yes."

"Who else was she seeing?" Brogan leaned closer. "I'll tear his head off."

I raised a hand. "I'm not giving you any details, not with the mood you're in. Take a breath, Brogan, and back off."

His hands clenched into fists. "I'll kill whoever did this."

"Maybe you've already killed tonight."

His nostrils expanded, and he stepped into my personal space. "You think I killed Flossie?"

"Did you catch her out on a lie?"

"No! I cared for her. She was the first woman I've been interested in making a life with for decades. Why would I kill her?"

I tried to shove him back, but he didn't move. "Because you found out she was seeing other people behind your back. You're proving to me right now that you've got a temper. You figured out what was going on and got revenge."

He hissed in my face, his eyes flashed and turned into deep, dark pools of rage. This vampire was about to lose control.

Magic sparked on the tips of my fingers. "We don't need to go there. You have to answer these questions. The angels will want to know exactly the same as I do. You knew Florentine. You were dating her. Maybe you figured out what she was really doing here and got angry."

"What do you mean, what she was really doing here? She was here for me." He growled deep in his chest. "We were making a life together."

"She was making a life with other guys," I said. "Florentine deceived you. She deceived her husband and the other man she was seeing. She's not an innocent party."

He tipped back his head, and an agonized howl slid from his lips.

I took the opportunity to put some distance between us but kept my magic primed just in case Brogan decided to take his anger out on me.

Two gusts of icy wind blasted from behind me, and I blinked as Granny Ana and Grandpa Cezar appeared on either side of Brogan.

Concern filtered across Granny Ana's face as she clamped a hand on his shoulder. "Whatever's the matter, child? We heard your cry for help."

Grandpa Cezar gripped Brogan's elbow. "Have you been hurt?"

Brogan sagged in their grip before wrapping his arms around Granny Ana and holding her tight.

She patted his shoulder as she whispered words of comfort in his ear before her gaze went to me, hardening as it did so. "What have you said to my grandson to make him behave this way?"

I licked my lips. Confronting three unhappy vampires was something no one would ever look forward to doing. "I was asking him a few questions about the woman he was dating."

"What about her?" Grandpa Cezar snapped.

The growl from Granny Ana sounded more beast than vampire. "How dare you upset Brogan like this?"

Wiggles and Bandit appeared on either side of me. Their fur was puffed out and their teeth bared as if they sensed the very real danger I was in.

I gestured for them both to stay where they were. One false move and this could get messy fast.

Brogan raised his head from his granny's shoulder, tears in his dark eyes. "Tempest thinks I'm a killer."

# Chapter 10

Granny Ana and Grandpa Cezar talked at once, speaking so rapidly I missed half of what they were saying.

"Slow down," I said. "I don't have vampire hearing. Normal speed talking only."

Granny Ana growled at me before sighing. "Brogan's no killer. He'd never do such a thing. We have the same honor code. We don't drink on our home territory. If this woman he was seeing was drained of blood, then you're looking at the wrong vampire."

"And I can assure you, neither of us drank from this woman," Grandpa Cezar said. "We respect the rules Brogan lives by and follow them when we're in his territory. We wouldn't wish to bring shame to the family name by breaking the rules."

"As happy as I am to hear that," I said, "Florentine wasn't drained of blood. She was held by magic first, then crushed by a wall."

Brogan groaned and dropped his head back on his granny's shoulder.

The death stare she gave me made me shudder. "It's not appropriate to talk about these things in front of my grandson. You must see how distressed he is. If he'd harmed this woman, he wouldn't be upset like this. He'd be celebrating."

"I don't know many people would think murdering someone worthy of a celebration," I said.

Grandpa Cezar and Granny Ana snarled at me and exposed their fangs in a threat display.

I lifted my chin, refusing to show how intimidated I felt. "Brogan was involved with this woman. Now she's dead. Questions have to be asked."

"But not now," Granny Ana said. "You can see he's in shock."

Brogan pulled himself upright and rubbed a hand down his face. "Tempest, I'm sorry. When I heard what happened to Flossie, I lost control. I didn't mean to rage at you. I understand you're only trying to help. I just, I mean, this is Flossie."

"She has a funny way of showing her help," Grandpa Cezar said.

"No, Grandpa. She's right to be here," Brogan said.

"I don't want to cause any trouble," I said. "Brogan, we're friends, but I have to know what's going on. The angels will be here in the morning asking the exact same questions, and they might be more suspicious of you than I am."

His shoulders slumped. "Dazielle's definitely not a fan of mine. If she thinks I'm involved, she'll come after me."

"What were you doing tonight?" I asked. "Did you see Florentine this evening?"

"Flossie, I mean, Florentine, no, I didn't see her." He tilted his head. "Although, I was unsettled. I could smell her around. She'd told me she wasn't going to be in the village for a couple of days, but I'd often get a strong scent as if she was somewhere close by."

"Was she staying in the village? Is that why you were picking up her smell?" I asked.

"No, she wasn't living in Willow Tree Falls. She was renting a room in a hotel outside the village," he said. "I thought it was strange at first, but Flossie said she was looking for somewhere to live and waiting for money to come through, so she could afford somewhere nice."

"Did she say where that money was coming from?" Maybe that was what she wanted from Lex and had been trying to find a way to get it from him without revealing herself.

"She didn't say." He scrubbed his eyes. "If things had continued to go so well between us, I was going to suggest she move in with me, so she wouldn't have any money worries."

"You didn't say anything about that," Granny Ana said.

"I was waiting for the right time." Brogan sighed. "Now there won't be a right time."

"That's enough for now," Granny Ana said. "We don't have long before the sun begins to rise. We must rest."

Being full vampires, Brogan's grandparents wouldn't do so well being out in the middle of the day.

"Brogan, before you go, what were you doing tonight?" I asked.

"I'm always out late," he said. "You know I like to go walking at night. You often see me drop by the club late in the evening. You're the only place that stays open late enough for me to enjoy."

"You were on your own?" I asked.

"We were with him," Granny Ana said. "Cezar and I were exploring the stone circle this evening. Brogan took us there, and we spent time linking into its curious power. You shouldn't ask where he was. We trust our grandson. He wouldn't do this. There's no logic behind you thinking he killed this woman."

I glanced at Brogan. There was, especially if he'd found out what Florentine was doing and let his temper loose on her.

"One more thing," I said. "I just want to know—"

"That's enough." Grandpa Cezar moved so quickly I didn't even see him until he was standing in front of me, glaring down. "We must retire."

Wiggles and Bandit growled at him.

A smirk crossed his stark, handsome face. "I understand you have power, witch. But do not test this family. We protect our own. We'd give our lives to protect our grandson."

"I'm glad to hear Brogan has people on his side. But if he's guilty, he needs to pay for what he's done," I said.

"Grandpa, it's okay," Brogan said. "I trust Tempest to do the right thing. She'll figure this out. She'll find out I'm innocent."

I risked a glance away from the scary vampire getting all up in my face. "Of course, I will."

"And you'll also find out what happened to Flossie." Brogan's words choked out of him.

After a few more seconds of glaring down at me with hatred in his eyes, Grandpa Cezar backed away. "Since my grandson tells me you can be trusted, then I must believe that. But tread carefully, Tempest. I will be watching you."

I just about managed not to shudder again. "I'll need to speak to you again, Brogan."

"I'll come by the club. We can talk then," he said. "I want this cleared up as much as you do."

With some reluctance, I nodded. It was getting late, and I was exhausted. "I'll catch up with you later." With another careful look at the grandparents to make sure they weren't about to tear me to shreds the second I turned my back, I walked away with Wiggles and Bandit, resisting the almost overwhelming urge to run as fast as I could.

As we rounded the bend and headed toward Cloven Hoof, I slowed. My stomach tightened, and I grimaced. We had company waiting for us.

Dazielle stood outside the main doors, her wings outstretched and her arms crossed over her chest. And from the look on her face, I was in big trouble.

"I figured as much," she said as we drew nearer.

"I don't know what you're talking about," I said.

"Sure you don't. So, you haven't just been talking to Brogan Costin about his involvement in Florentine's murder?"

"We may have bumped into each other," I said. "There's no crime in that."

"You went looking for him." She stepped aside as I unlocked the door.

"You didn't say I couldn't do that." I glanced over my shoulder. "Are you coming in or simply going to stand out here and glower at me?" I didn't wait for an answer as I strode in with Wiggles and Bandit beside me.

The sound of the door being pulled open and footsteps following me confirmed she was coming in.

I had no plans to grovel over what I'd done, but if we were working together, maybe I should keep things civil.

I walked behind the bar, selected the finest Peruvian dried mushrooms we had in stock, and poured two generous shots of lemon drops before gesturing to a booth.

Dazielle raised her eyebrows before walking over and settling in a seat.

"I smell leftovers." Wiggles' nose pointed toward the kitchen. "I'm going to see what Chef's left behind."

"Don't make yourself sick gorging on everything," I said as he trotted off to the kitchen. I glanced at Bandit. "Thanks for your help tonight. You should get back to Aurora."

She eyed Dazielle. "I guess my work is done. And Aurora will be missing me."

"Tell her I'll drop by and see her soon."

Bandit nodded. She stood, flicked her tail, and left the bar.

I sat opposite Dazielle and sipped my drink, waiting for her to begin the interrogation.

She stared at me levelly for several seconds before taking a mushroom and popping it into her mouth. "I'm making arrangements to have Florentine's body exhumed. That should tell us if there's been some mistake in her identification."

"Good idea," I said. "Although Lex seems certain he buried his wife, we need to be sure. Grief makes people see and do odd things."

"Like misidentify a loved one?"

"It's possible."

She arched an eyebrow. "The woman we found in the castle grounds does match Florentine Fontaine's physical appearance, but she's not in our system, so we can't run any fingerprint analysis."

"And she's definitely dead this time?" I asked.

"You checked her. Besides, Cassiel knows how to identify a dead body."

I raised a hand. "I'm not saying she doesn't, but it won't be the first time a dead body has gotten up and walked out of your morgue. Plus, there are spells that make a person appear dead. There are also potions somebody can drink to slow the heartbeat to an undetectable level."

"Duly noted."

I repressed a sigh. "Maybe that's what Florentine did the first time. This could be a big ruse she's trying to pull off."

"For what reason?"

"I'm thinking it has to do with her husband," I said. "Lex has been troubled by what he believed was a demon. What if it wasn't a demon but his supposedly dead wife?"

"What's she hoping to achieve by doing that?"

"Lex could be hiding things about their marriage," I said. "He admitted that things weren't good between them. Florentine was having money troubles and possibly being unfaithful."

"Why would that make her fake her own death?" Dazielle asked.

"To get out of a toxic situation," I said. "To get rid of a husband who was causing her problems and start again? Maybe her new life wasn't all she thought it would be, or she ran out of money, so she decided to return to Lex and get what she thought she was owed."

"That's a lot of assumptions," she said. "We've yet to prove this is even the real Florentine." She drank some of her lemon drop and ate more mushrooms.

"Whoever it is, someone killed her."

Dazielle nodded. "We have the obvious suspect with Lex Fontaine. Assuming it was Florentine found under the fallen wall, I always put the partner of the deceased at the top of the list of killers."

"He's on my list too," I said. "But there's also Gregor. His confession that he dated Florentine also has to put him in the frame."

"Their meeting can't be a coincidence," Dazielle said. "He gets the job working at the castle, and at the exact same time, Florentine appears and makes him fall for her."

"My thoughts exactly," I said. "She targeted Gregor because she wanted something from him. It could have been information about Lex, or she might have wanted something inside the castle. When Gregor showed her around, he said she was interested in finding places where things might have been altered or changed. Walls that were knocked down, that sort of thing."

"What did she want from the castle?" Dazielle asked.

"Something her husband wasn't willing to give her," I said. "Lex said Florentine was greedy."

"You're thinking Gregor discovered who Florentine really was and attacked her in a jealous rage?"

"Gregor doesn't strike me as the kind of guy who'd lose control of his temper," I said. "Mind you, neither does Lex, but Gregor loved Florentine. He was heartbroken when she was discovered. Maybe those intense emotions sent him over the edge. Florentine lied and deceived him, and she was cheating on him with Brogan."

"And neither Gregor nor Lex have good alibis for the time of the murder," Dazielle said.

I nodded. "They were both alone. Either of them could have gone into the grounds and killed Florentine."

"Jinn and elven magic does have an old quality to it, just as we discovered on the body," Dazielle said. "They're plausible suspects, but we also have Brogan to consider. Since you went behind my back and spoke to him, what did he tell you about his involvement with Florentine?"

I let that little dig slide by without comment. "She called herself Flossie Burnett when they met. She was lying to him too."

"So, she goes by Florentine, Fay, and Flossie. I'll run those names through our systems and see if anything comes up. Were they close?"

"I'd say so. Brogan was devastated when he discovered what had happened. It sounded like things were serious between them, and that's a big deal coming from him."

"Brogan Costin's a player when it comes to the ladies," she said. "I never imagined him as the settling type."

"Exactly. He was talking about moving her in with him. Apparently, Florentine had been staying in a hotel outside the village. She was waiting for some money to come through."

"Money she was going to steal from Lex once she'd sent him crazy by making him think he was being stalked by a demon?"

"That could work. Florentine gets Lex committed for observation due to his fragile mental state. It would give her a chance to ransack the castle and find exactly what she was after."

"Which means, Brogan has the same motive for wanting her dead as Gregor," Dazielle said. "He discovered she was lying to him and seeing someone else and decided it had to stop."

"I'd stand next to Brogan and support him over most things, but he does have a temper," I said. "His vampire urges can take over. Given his intense feelings for Florentine, maybe something snapped. He may have seen her with Lex or Gregor or even learned the truth about her identity."

"And was pushed over the edge into killing her." Dazielle finished her lemon drop. "And again, vampire energy has that old flavor to it. It would fit the crime scene evidence. Did he tell you where he was when the murder took place?"

"He's got his grandparents visiting," I said. "He was with them at the stone circle."

"That's a better alibi than the other two," she said. "But all three suspects could have wanted this man-eater dead. I'm not discounting anyone for now. Although, I'll look particularly closely at Lex to begin with."

"I'd pick him as top suspect too," I said.

"We're actually agreeing on something?" She smirked. "This day just keeps getting weirder. A dead woman returns to life then dies again. And now, Tempest Crypt's on my side."

"Hey! I'm not always fighting you," I said. "When you're not talking garbage and making ridiculous accusations against me, I don't mind you. Even if you do shed feathers all the time." I flicked a white piece of downy feather off the table.

"What a charming endorsement of our relationship," she said.

"Like you don't think the same about me."

She lifted one shoulder. "You have your moments. You can be both useful and intensely irritating."

"Right back at you." I chewed on a mushroom and let the mellow, tangy flavor soothe me. "What's your next move going to be with Lex?"

"We won't have any information about Florentine's exhumation until at least lunchtime," she said. "While that's being done, I'll have somebody speak to Brogan and confirm what you've told me. When the details of Florentine's remains come back, I'll bring Lex in for more formal questioning. If it turns out he buried the wrong woman the first time around, that will raise a whole host of new questions."

"Like did he lie when he identified her body? If so, what reason does he have for deliberately burying the wrong woman and claiming she was his wife?"

"Among other things," Dazielle said.

"If Lex wasn't involved, it could mean that Florentine was behind all this. She killed an innocent woman to fake her death in the landslide."

Dazielle's nose wrinkled. "The more I learn about Florentine Fontaine, the less I like her."

"The feeling's mutual," I said. "She was trouble."

"There you go again, agreeing with me. At this rate, I'll have to start calling you a friend."

"Let's not get ahead of ourselves," I said with a smile.

We sat for a few seconds in a companionable silence and ate more mushrooms. Working with Dazielle wasn't so terrible. When she wasn't being uptight and officious, she did have a decent brain inside that pretty head of hers.

She shifted in her seat and pulled a file out from behind her before setting it on the table.

"What's that?" I asked.

"While you were sneaking around questioning Brogan, I went back to Angel Force. This file contains information on your dad."

The mushroom I held slipped from my fingers, and my heart skipped a beat. "You have a file on my dad?"

She nodded. "You've been asking around about him. I haven't forgotten that you questioned me a few months ago to see if there was anything I knew. I thought it was odd at the time. So, I did some digging. There was an investigation into what happened when he disappeared."

I reached for the file, a slight tremor in my hand. "I know about that, but I've never seen any of the paperwork. Your old boss told me it wasn't available for public viewing."

"Don't get your hopes up. The information in this file is old, but I figured it might give you some closure, if nothing else. You'll see that everything was done to locate him. The information also suggests that nothing bad happened to him. I don't know if that's any comfort."

My eyes misted as I rested my hand on the file and pulled it closer. I opened it and stared at the contents, but I couldn't process the words.

Dazielle cleared her throat. "This must be difficult for you, Tempest. Are you sure you want to rake up the past? Your dad's been gone a long time. Why are you looking for him now?"

I swallowed the lump in my throat. "I need to see Foxglove Shadowsoul."

Her eyebrows leaped up. "Not a chance."

I sucked in a breath. "She's my source of information. The last time I saw her, she told me my dad was still alive."

Sympathy crossed Dazielle's face. "You can't believe her. Foxglove's a deviant and a liar. She was planning to bring down the Magic Council. There's not a thread of good within that monster."

I pressed my fingers against my temple. "What if this one time she was telling the truth?"

"She'd have said anything to save her miserable existence," Dazielle said. "I recall from your statement that you were about to kill her. Frank was in control and choking the life out of Foxglove. She must have known that your dad disappeared and grabbed onto the possibility that you'd save her life by telling you what you wanted to hear."

I squeezed my eyes shut. "I can't stop thinking about it."

Dazielle blew out a quiet breath. "I understand. But going to see Foxglove won't make this any better. She won't have answers for you. She'll mess with your head just for fun."

"It will make it better for me." I opened my eyes. "I'll convince her to tell the truth. I'll know if she's lying. But I have to figure this out. This file of information might have something in it, but I need more recent facts. Foxglove might have that." And I'd had confirmation from Isaac Dubrov that my dad was still out there. I wasn't letting this go.

"She doesn't. She had hollow promises that'll leave you in a worse position than you already are."

"That's my choice," I said. "I know what I'm getting into. I'm prepared for her to mess with me. I can handle it."

"I can't permit a visit."

I stared straight at her. "Dazielle, I've never begged you for anything. But please, I'm begging you now. I have to see Foxglove. You know where she is. You can arrange a visit."

"Of course, I do." She sighed. "And despite what you think, it gives me no comfort to hear you beg."

"I'm feeling sick to my very boots for doing it," I said. "But this is how serious I am. A short visit, that's all I ask."

"Will you leave this alone after that?"

I wasn't sure I could, but maybe this was all I needed to convince myself Dad was still alive or dead. I had to know what happened to him. This was my chance to put this mystery to bed. "Yes, I won't ask to see her again."

"I'm promising nothing," Dazielle said. "But I'll make inquiries and see if she'd be receptive to a visit."

"Thank you," I breathed out. "That's all I want."

"That's no small request, you know," she said sharply.

"I'm sure you'll keep reminding me of that," I said.

Dazielle slid from the booth. She patted my shoulder. "Get some sleep, Tempest. When the sun comes up, we have a killer to catch."

I watched her go as I sank against the cushioned booth seat. We did, and I actually thought that together we could do it. But I also had a missing father to find, and I needed to do that on my own.

# Chapter 11

A persistent prodding on my arm roused me from my sleep. I rolled over and fell off the couch, giving a grunt of surprise as I hit the floor.

Wiggles skipped out of the way to avoid being squashed as I landed. "What are you doing sleeping on there?"

I grimaced as I pushed myself to my knees. "I was up late reading. I must have dozed off."

"What are you reading?" He nosed a piece of paper from the file I'd spread out around me.

I scrambled to gather the pieces of paper. I'd managed a few hours of sleep but not much, having spent most of the night looking through the file Dazielle had given me about my dad.

"There's nothing here that would interest you," I said, "just a boring case file."

Wiggles' red eyes narrowed. "So boring you had to look at it all night?"

I sighed as I sank back on the couch, the papers gripped in my hands. "I'm looking for... I didn't want to say anything until I knew for sure."

He hopped onto the couch and placed his front paws on my knees. "Sure about what?"

I sighed and rested my head back. "You weren't in the room the night I captured Foxglove in the castle."

"That's right. I was being a superhero and rescuing a damsel in distress. Why's that important?"

I smoothed down my messy hair. "I was out of control. Frank was in charge, and he was enjoying choking Foxglove."

"You probably enjoyed that a bit as well."

I snorted a laugh. "Maybe a little. Anyway, the only thing that saved her was when Foxglove said she had information about my dad."

Wiggles' ears shot up. "What does she know?"

"That's just it; she didn't tell me. And before I had the chance to find out more, Frank got back in on the action, then Axel wrapped Foxglove up in flames. But she told me he's alive."

He shook his head. "You can't believe her."

I ran a hand down my face and held up the papers. "I need to know for sure. Last night, Dazielle gave me this old file full of information gathered after Dad went missing."

"Is there anything useful in there?"

"Not really. It only told me what I already know, although it does detail that the angels looked for him for several weeks before moving it to a cold case. It was like he just vanished. One day he was here, and the next he'd walked out the front door, and that was it. He was gone."

"Did the angels draw any conclusions about what happened to him?"

"Nothing. Although, on the positive side, they didn't find any evidence that he was hurt, which means he could still be alive, just like Foxglove claims."

He sniffed my nose and licked my cheek. "I'm hurt."

"About what?"

"That you left me out of this."

"Wiggles, this isn't about you. I need—"

"I loved him too," he said. "And I want to help you find him. If he's out there, we need to know what's going on."

A rush of affection hit me, and I wrapped my arms around Wiggles.

"Calm down. This moment doesn't call for cuddles. You know I don't like them."

"Then suck it up, because I need a hug." I rested my chin on his back as he endured the cuddle. "I didn't mean to exclude you, but there's no point in telling anyone what I'm doing until I find evidence. One way or the other, I have to know what happened."

"You've not told anybody else?" He squirmed out of my arms and stepped back.

"Not even Aurora," I said. "The only person who knows anything about this is Foxglove. And Dazielle. But she's only included because I want her to fix up a meeting between Foxglove and me."

He snorted. "You shouldn't go anywhere near Foxglove."

"I don't want to," I said, "but I'm not giving up on this."

"Then we're in this together," he said. "Providing you supply me with an endless amount of doughnuts to give me enough energy, I'll take on this search for your dad."

"You'll do anything for doughnuts," I said.

"Naturally. They're my one true love." He licked my fingers. "Well, one of them."

"You have to keep this a secret," I said. "You mustn't tell anybody else, especially not Aurora, not yet."

"Don't you think she should know?"

"And build her hopes up that our dad could still be alive?" I shook my head. "She's been through too much recently. But imagine if I find him and bring him back to Willow Tree Falls. She'll be so happy."

"And annoyed with you that you didn't tell her what you've been up to."

"An annoyed Aurora I can handle," I said. "Besides, she'll forget about it in five minutes once Dad's home."

He tilted his head from side to side. "I don't want you to be disappointed if your search comes to nothing. I remember how sad you were when he disappeared. You used to cry into my fur when you thought nobody could hear you."

"I'm surprised you remember that," I said. "It was years ago." I'd spent a lot of nights wondering what had happened to my dad. Wiggles had always been there, at the time a regular dog and not the wisecracking goofball I had now. He'd endured all my hugs and the tear-stained nights as I'd wondered if I'd done something to drive my dad away.

He hopped up, resting his paws against my shoulders. "Whatever happens, I've got your back."

I tried to hug him again, but he bounced off the couch and trotted away, his tail up.

"That's your hug quota for the month."

I chuckled as I stood and headed to the bathroom. I was happy to have his help. Doing this felt like a massive task. With Wiggles by my side, it suddenly seemed a lot more positive.

After a quick shower and breakfast, we headed to Angel Force.

Dominic was behind the desk when we walked in, and he grinned brightly at me.

"Morning, Tempest. I hear we're working together to crack this murder case wide open."

"Dazielle's actually telling people we're working together?" I shook my head as I smiled. Wonders would never cease.

"It's all got us stumped." He scrubbed a hand over his chin. "Demons, dead wives, all those boyfriends being hidden away. The poor woman must have been exhausted by going on so many dates and making sure she didn't get her boyfriends' names mixed up."

I chuckled as I nodded at the door behind Dominic. "Since we're working together, is it okay if I go through?"

"I don't see why not," he said. "Want a coffee?"

"You're an angel, literally." I squeezed his arm as I walked past with Wiggles.

The office was bustling with activity. Everyone looked hard at work, and it took me a couple of minutes to spot Dazielle among all the fluttering wings.

She lifted a chin when she saw me and gestured me over. "Good night?" She arched an eyebrow.

"I've had worse," I said. "Have you made any progress with Florentine's murder?"

"We're still waiting for information on who was buried in Florentine's coffin," she said. "It shouldn't be more than a few hours until we know exactly who was in there. I'm sending Jophiel and Dominic out to speak to store owners and see if they can confirm seeing Florentine around the village in the lead up to her death."

I nodded a thanks at Dominic as he brought over two coffees for us. "Sounds like a good plan." I grabbed Wiggles' collar just before he stole a cookie off the desk of an angel.

Dazielle's lips pursed, and she shook her head. "He's supposed to wait in the reception. None of the angels trust him."

"He's basically a decent hellhound. He simply has no control around food," I said.

"That cookie is sitting there feeling unloved," Wiggles said. "I want to show it a whole lot of love."

Dazielle glowered at him. "Anyway, I have a job for you in this investigation."

"What's that?" I asked.

"Since you already know your way around the castle and Lex trusts you, you need to get back there."

"You want me to speak to Lex?"

"Not Lex," she said. "I've spoken to him already this morning. He's agreed to come to the station later for questioning. So far, I haven't mentioned that we've got him as our prime suspect."

"What's all this *we* business?" Wiggles muttered, his gaze still on the unloved cookie.

I winked at him before turning back to Dazielle. "What do you want me to do at the castle?"

"Interview the ghosts."

My mouth dropped open. "You're kidding? Ghosts are so... flighty. There's no substance to them."

"That comes with being a ghost," Dazielle said. "They live in the castle. They see what goes on, which means they could have useful information about what happened to Florentine and if Lex is involved in her murder."

My nose wrinkled. The trouble with ghosts was that they were so flimsy. They floated about in the ethereal plane with one foot in the world of the living and the other in the land of the dead. Their thoughts and memories flipped from one decade to the next with startling speed. You never knew if they were talking about something that happened yesterday or twenty years ago.

"We're wasting our time with the ghosts," I said. "They won't be reliable witnesses."

"They could be," Dazielle said.

"There must be dozens of ghosts in the castle."

"And your job is to speak to them all. Discount those who know nothing about Florentine or pay no attention to Lex. Concentrate on the ones who like hanging around the living."

I tipped my head back and groaned. It would take days to get through all the ghosts.

Dazielle was silent for a few seconds. "If you do it, I'll get you in to see Foxglove."

My eyes narrowed. "That's a bribe."

"It's an incentive," she said. "You deal with the ghosts and help keep Lex calm, and I'll fix up a meeting with Foxglove as soon as possible."

It was horribly unfair the way she was twisting my arm, but she knew my weak spot. I'd do anything to see Foxglove, even spend a few days being frozen, chased, and aggravated by ghosts.

"I'll do it," I said. "But you have to guarantee me that I get that meeting."

She nodded. "You'll get it."

"It's a deal. When do you want me to speak to the ghosts?"

"Now's looking good."

With a sigh, I downed my coffee. "I'll get right on it." I headed out of Angel Force with Wiggles, and we walked toward Castle Falls.

"Hey! Wait up!"

I turned and smiled as Aurora hurried toward me.

"I've heard the news about what's happening at Castle Falls. Is it true?" she asked.

"That depends on what you've been told." It was good to see the gossip mill was functioning smoothly in the village.

She looked around and leaned closer. "Lex's wife is back. Or rather, she was. And she was murdered near the castle."

"That's about right."

"Lex must be so confused. I'm confused!"

"He's finding it hard to believe that his wife, who was supposed to have been dead for two years, was most likely alive this whole time. It's a bit of a mess."

"I can imagine," she said. "Lex must need comforting."

"Are you going to be the one to offer him comfort?" I grinned at her.

Her blue eyes sparkled. "I hate to think of him all alone in that big castle, worrying about what happened."

"Yeah, I bet he's really worried. Worried he might go to jail. You might want to rethink offering comfort to Lex. He's a murder suspect."

Her hand flew to her mouth, and she took a step back. "He's really a suspect? Why?"

"Let's think about that for a second," I said. "The victim was found in his grounds. He was married to her, and they didn't have a good relationship, and she was seeing two other guys behind his back."

"Oh! That does rather change things," she said. "Still, Lex is a sweetheart. This must all be a misunderstanding. I can't picture him as a killer."

"Then reframe your thoughts when it comes to Lex Fontaine being your new knight in shining armor. Dazielle's very interested in him as the killer."

Aurora tilted her head. "Since when did you listen to Dazielle?"

I lifted a shoulder. "Since we've been working together on this case. She's proving to be not so annoying this time around. I doubt it'll last."

Her eyes widened as she stared at me in mock surprise. "Tempest Crypt, officially working with the angels. Have you had a bump on the head?"

"Funny girl," I said. "Haven't you got a store to run?"

She looked over her shoulder. "I do need to get back. I left several customers in there, although Bandit's keeping an eye on things. Keep me informed about what's going on. And the second you know Lex is innocent, tell me."

"So you can be first in line to date him?"

She poked her tongue out at me. "If he's lucky."

I chuckled as I walked the rest of the way to the castle with Wiggles. Aurora deserved happiness, but there was no way I was letting Lex loose on her until I'd confirmed he hadn't killed Florentine.

The door to the castle was open as I reached it.

I peered around the side. "Is anybody home?"

A moment later, Martha appeared. "Miss Crypt. May I help you?"

"I hope so," I said. "I'm looking for Lex. Is he about?"

She walked closer, her hands clasped behind her back. "He's resting at the moment. Between you and me, he's not in a good place. Finding his wife dead again has rather unsettled him."

"No kidding," I said. "Did you know her?"

"I did," Martha said. "She wasn't the easiest of women to work for. I took most of my instructions from Mr. Fontaine, while Florentine tended to issue orders and then pretend I was invisible unless I did something to displease her. Then I'd get the sharp end of her tongue."

"You didn't like her?"

"I form no opinion about my employers," she said. "Providing they pay my wages and give me comfortable accommodation, I'm here to serve them as they require."

Did serving her employer expand to murder? Could Lex have gotten Martha involved in this mystery? "Have the angels asked you where you were on the night of Florentine's murder?"

She drew herself up and cupped her hands under her ample bosom. "In bed asleep. I sleep alone before you ask, so I don't have anyone to back that up, but I had nothing to gain from getting rid of Mrs. Fontaine. I'm still trying to get my head around the fact she wasn't in the coffin she was originally placed in. I attended the funeral. I might not have cared for her manners, but as far as I was concerned, she was already dead."

"Yes. That has got everyone stumped," I said.

"Is there anything else I can help you with?" Martha asked. "I really don't want to disturb Mr. Fontaine unless it's essential to speak with him."

"You might be able to. I'm not really here to see Lex."

"Who are you here to see?"

"The castle's ghosts," I said. "Any chance you can fix me up with some interviews?"

She sniffed before turning and walking away. "Follow me. You'll need some strong coffee and cookies if you're going to deal with our ghosts."

Anyone who offered cookies was decent in my book. Despite Martha's abruptness, I was warming to her.

I rubbed my hands together and nodded at Wiggles. It was time to talk to some ghosts.

# Chapter 12

"If you scream in my ear one more time, I'm going to have you exorcised." I glared into the glowing green eyes of the ghost who'd been alternating between whispering and screaming for the last ten minutes.

She floated in front of me, her long pale hair drifting around her like the tendrils of a Medusa.

"Where were you on the night of Florentine's murder?" I asked again.

She swirled around the room, making me shiver and the hairs on my arm stand up as the temperature plummeted.

I snagged the last cherry and chocolate cookie off the plate and munched on it as I waited for her to stop spinning. Ghosts, they were so annoying.

"This one's a bust," Wiggles said. He lay sprawled on the rug in front of the stone fireplace. "She's wasting our time."

"Our time? You've been asleep for five hours."

"I've been listening this whole time. I just had my eyes closed. I don't need them open to know this ghost is a pest, just like the others."

The ghost homed in on him and swept over his head.

"And she can stop doing that." He growled and snapped at the air as she passed him again.

The ghost gave one more scream before disappearing through the wall.

That made fifteen ghosts interviewed, and zero useful information coming from any of them. I wondered if Dazielle had set this up just so I'd fail and stay out of her way while she ran this case.

I rubbed my aching forehead and drank the last of my coffee. It wasn't only the ghosts causing me problems. I was struggling to focus as I continued to think about my dad and the possibility of getting in to see Foxglove.

I needed to focus. "Who's next in line for a pointless interrogation?" Martha had supplied a list of the house ghosts who'd been sighted since moving into the castle. There were forty in total, and the next ghost on the list was the gray lady.

I stood and cleared my throat. I was no ghost whisperer, but they usually came when you called their name, providing they were in a good enough mood to want to deal with the living. "Gray lady, we request your presence in the living room."

Martha had warned me the ghosts liked to be spoken to politely. She'd experienced what happened if you got sharp with them. They'd sabotaged her dinner one night by swapping out the sugar for salt, and she almost killed Lex when she'd offered him a salt laden plum pudding.

Wiggles hopped to his feet as a shimmering image materialized.

The gray lady was just as her title suggested. She was wispy, pale gray, her hair tucked neatly under an old-fashioned looking cloth cap and her skirts down to her ankles.

"I'm Tempest, and this is Wiggles," I said. "We're interviewing the house ghosts about what happened the night Lex found the body in the grounds. Were you here at the time?"

She nodded.

"Did you see anything going on in the grounds?"

She shook her head. "I do not leave the castle. This is my home."

"What were you doing when the body was discovered?"

"I like to float around the passages."

"The hallway?"

"No, the castle's passages. Very few know they exist. It's why I like them. You don't get disturbed."

Wiggles trotted over, his ears up. "Are these secret passages? We have to check those out."

"Where do they go?" I asked.

"All around the castle," she said. "There are several rooms they lead to. The new castle owner often uses them."

"What for?"

"I can show you," the gray lady said.

This ghost seemed friendly, but I needed to be cautious I wasn't about to walk into a trap, and she wouldn't morph into some scary harridan and trap me in the castle walls.

"How do we get to these passages?" I asked. "We can't move through walls like you."

She smiled and inclined her head. "Neither can the castle's new master. Walk to the right-hand side of the fireplace. You'll discover a small hole. Push your fingers in and pull the lever. That opens the door. That's how he gains access."

I did just that and discovered a hole big enough to shove three fingers through. I felt around and located a lever. It was stiff, but after a couple of tugs, something clicked, and a section of wall opened to my right. I eased my fingers in behind it and pulled it open.

"This way," the gray lady said before floating through the wall and out of sight.

I scribbled a note on the list of ghosts. *Inside the castle walls. If we don't return in an hour, get help.*

That would cover our backs if this ghost turned nasty. And if the worst happened, at least our corpses could be recovered and not lost forever in the hidden passages.

I cast a small ball of light as we headed into the dark tunnel.

Wiggles followed close to my heels as the ghost glided in front of us. "What's Lex doing creeping around these old tunnels?" he whispered.

"We're about to find out," I said. "Whatever it is, he doesn't want anyone to know about it."

The ghost drifted around a corner, and I hurried to keep up with her.

"What's your real name?" I asked her.

She looked back over her shoulder. "I've been known as the gray lady for so long, I almost forget. When I was living, I was called Caroline."

"Did you work at the castle?"

"I did. And I like the title, lady, I've been given since my death. I was a maid in the kitchens. No one ever thought I was a lady when I was alive."

"And you died here? Is that why you haunt the place?"

"That's correct," she said. "This is my home. Whether I'm alive or dead, it's the only place I ever felt happy. I had a purpose here. A role. I don't want to leave. We're not far now. Keep up."

Wiggles trotted alongside me, chewing on something.

"Please don't tell me you ate food you found in here?"

"It was a really big spider," he said. "I did it for your benefit. You did not want this beast dropping on your head. It punched me on the nose when I made a grab for it."

I shuddered. There was bound to be all kinds of things creeping around in the dark down here, big spiders included.

The gray lady hovered by a bend in the passageway. "This is where the castle's master often visits." She drifted to one side.

I stepped into the large room, and my eyes widened as I looked around. It was crammed full of gold coins, jewelry, gemstones, and all manner of treasure.

"He lied to us!" Wiggles bounded around the room, sniffing everything. "Lex said he didn't have a hoard of treasure."

"I should have known better than to believe him," I said. "This is typical jinn behavior. They always have to hoard their riches. They can never have enough of the glittering stuff." I followed after Wiggles, running my fingers over the stacks of gold coins and inspecting a few heavy chalices studded with gems.

"Look at this!" Wiggles bounded over to a pile of old lamps. "One of these has to be his."

"Lex isn't that kind of jinn. He said he doesn't have the ability to grant wishes."

Wiggles furiously rubbed his face against the lamps. "Yeah, and he also said he didn't have any treasure."

My mouth twisted to the side. I'd believed Lex when he told me he didn't have a treasure hoard and couldn't grant wishes. He was so good at lying, perhaps he'd lied about other things, such as what happened to his wife and how much he really knew about her murder.

"I'm going to rub every single one of these lamps," Wiggles said. "Then I'll be guaranteed my three wishes."

"If Lex has a lamp that allows him to grant wishes, he's not going to leave it lying around for anyone to get their hands on."

"No one else knows about this place." Wiggles flopped onto the lamps and rolled around. "This is the perfect hiding spot. I bet his lamp's mixed up in this pile, so no one knows which one to choose."

I looked at the gray lady, who waited patiently by the door. "When did Lex move his treasures in here?"

"The first day he moved in," she said. "He did it at night."

"When no one else was about and wouldn't see what he was doing," I said. "Was he alone?"

"No one helped. It took him several nights to bring everything in," the gray lady said.

I walked around the room. "What if Florentine faked her death the first time, so she could get her hands on this treasure?"

"I don't get it," Wiggles said as he rubbed himself against even more lamps. "Why pretend to be dead to get this treasure?"

"Lex could have denied having it, just like he did with us. He hid it from her, so she couldn't hoard it herself or fritter it away. Florentine faked her own death and then watched Lex, waiting to discover where he was hiding his treasure."

"For two years?"

"Maybe this was the first time he'd moved it," I said. "She bided her time and kept an eye on what Lex was doing. Then, he moved into the castle, and she knew his treasure would come with him."

"And pretended to be a demon to drive him away and get the treasures denied her when they were together," Wiggles said. "That's kind of smart. A bit crazy, but clever."

"Have you seen anyone else come in here?" I asked the gray lady.

"Only the white demon," she said.

"Who's the white demon?"

"She often follows Lex. She watches him all the time. The nights he moved his hoard of treasure here, she snuck in and saw what he was doing."

"Why do you call her the white demon?" I asked.

"She conceals her identity under a flare of magic. But she has long white hair. She would taunt Lex at night. She's not a kind spirit. That's why I call her a demon."

"That must have been Florentine," I said. "We have to speak to Lex. This is the reason she was hounding him. She planned to drive him mad, chase him from the castle, and claim all of this as hers."

"Leave me here," Wiggles said. "I've got a few hundred more lamps to rub."

"That's enough grinding all over those lamps," I said. "Lex isn't going to grant you any wishes."

"You should rub some too," he said. "You'll gift a wish to me if you get lucky, won't you?"

"If I had a wish, it would be to stop you messing with those lamps."

"Would you like to see the rest of the passages?" the gray lady asked. "There are more treasures in the different rooms."

"Which means more lamps," Wiggles said. "I'll take a look."

"No, you won't," I said. "We need to get out of here and confront Lex about this."

"I can lead you back." The gray lady drifted out of the room and back down the passageway we'd walked along.

She slid through the wall, and I pushed open the door and stepped into the living room.

My heart thudded, and I slowed. Lex was waiting in the middle of the room. He stood with his hands folded behind him and his back erect.

"Hey, Lex," I said. "One of your ghosts showed us the secret passageways in the castle. You've got some explaining to do."

He paid me no attention as Wiggles bounded through the door. He bowed low to Wiggles. "What is your first wish?"

# Chapter 13

My eyebrows shot up as I stared at Lex. "His first what?"

Lex slowly lifted himself from his bow. "Your hellhound has rubbed my lamp. He gets his three wishes."

Wiggles bounced in the air. "I knew it! I figured one of them had to be yours."

I narrowed my eyes at Lex. "You told us you don't have the ability to grant wishes."

He sighed. "If you had this ability, would you seriously tell anybody? Can you imagine how many people try to find my lamp and use it to get their wishes?"

"That must get annoying," I said. "But isn't that what jinns are meant to do?"

"Yes! But it's highly inconvenient. When someone rubs my lamp, I have to come to them. No matter if I'm in the middle of something important, I must abandon it and attend to the person who's captured my wish interest. If they request my presence, then I appear."

"What should my first wish be?" Wiggles asked. "There's so much I want. Pizza for the rest of my life? Or maybe all-you-can-eat doughnuts every day?"

"If you would like to wish for one of those items, it will be yours," Lex said.

Wiggles sucked in a deep breath.

"Let's put a hold on granting wishes for now," I said. "We still have your wife's murder to solve."

"Until the wishes are dispensed, I won't be able to concentrate on anything else," Lex said. "My focus must be on the person whose wishes need to be granted."

"My own personal genie. This just keeps getting better," Wiggles said.

A frown flickered across Lex's face. "I would appreciate it if you make your wishes quickly. I have my wife's murder to resolve and an enormous castle to renovate."

"Let's all take a seat," I said. Lex had been caught lying twice now. He'd lied about his ability to grant wishes, which I could understand, but he'd also lied about his treasure hoard. Maybe he'd lied about his alibi at the time of his wife's death, on both occasions.

"I could wish for a harem," Wiggles said.

"No harem of dogs," I muttered. "Where would you keep them?"

"They can stay in the apartment with us," he said.

"Before you make any wishes, run them by me," I said. "I don't want to end up with an apartment full of dogs and the cabinets overflowing with doughnuts because you make the wrong wish."

"Both of those wishes are excellent," Wiggles said. "And they're my wishes. I can pick anything, can't I?" He turned to look at Lex.

"There are a few things you need to know about the wishes you've been granted," he said.

"Can we do the wish rules another time?" I asked. "We have the not insignificant problem of your dead wife to deal with."

He nodded. "Of course we do, but I must share this information with Wiggles. It's important he knows the responsibility that comes with having three wishes."

I slumped back on the couch. With Wiggles and Lex focused only on the wishes, my questions weren't getting answered anytime soon. "Go ahead."

Wiggles sat in front of Lex, his ears up. "What do I need to know?"

"When you've made a decision on the wish you would like, you must say, my first wish will be, and then state your wish. You'll get a single wish granted. When you'd like a second wish granted, you simply need to say—"

"My second wish is and whatever I want," Wiggles said. "Got it. Anything else?"

"Your wishes can't do harm to another person. As I've mentioned, there are gray areas concerning this, but keep your wishes positive and there shouldn't be any problem in having them granted."

"I don't think I've got anyone in my life I'd like to kill," Wiggles said. "Although, Bandit's probably up there most weeks."

Lex glanced at me. "You can also not ask for more than one thing at a time. So, you cannot say I wish for a new car, a million dollars, a harem of dogs, and free doughnuts for life under one wish. They would all be separate wishes."

"Could I ask for a car made out of doughnuts?" Wiggles asked.

I shut my eyes and groaned.

"It's just a thought," Wiggles said. "That could be fun. We can drive and eat at the same time."

"You may ask for that wish," Lex said. "Many people take time to consider their wishes before they ask them. You don't want to wish for something and then regret it. Once a wish is cast, it cannot be undone."

"I don't think anyone would regret having an endless supply of doughnuts in their life," Wiggles said.

"That's everything," Lex said. He settled his hands in his lap and glanced at me. "I'm assuming you've seen all my treasure?"

"Only one room," I said. "That was enough. Why didn't you tell the truth about your hoard?"

"For the same reason I didn't tell you about my wish ability," he said. "If people know I have a treasure hoard, I become a target. They either want to see it, steal it, or trade something for it. I don't want that. I want a quiet life. I want to be happy in my castle, surrounded by my treasures. It's here for my enjoyment, no one else's."

"Did you lie to Florentine about having no treasure?" I asked.

"Of course! She'd have spent her entire time hunting for it if she knew I had it. She'd have constantly nagged me. I would never share what I had with her."

"Which is why she came back," I said.

Lex's hand went to his mouth. "She discovered my treasure?"

"From my understanding of jinn, you'd be willing to do a lot to get your hands on a hoard of treasure like that," I said. "Would that include waiting two years for the right time to strike?"

He rubbed his forehead before nodding. "There's not much we wouldn't do in order to secure such a bounty."

"Although I don't have anything conclusive to go on, you said the demon bothering intensified since you moved here. According to your gray lady ghost, she saw a white demon follow you when you moved your treasure. I think that demon was Florentine. Or rather, Florentine pretending to be a demon."

Lex's lips pursed. "She always suspected I was hiding something. She tried to pretend she didn't care, but it's an obsession for us. Once we learn there's treasure almost within our reach, we have to find it. Nothing else matters."

"And Florentine decided she wanted the treasure more than she wanted to remain married to you," I said. "She faked her death and has been waiting all this time to see where you hid the treasure."

He groaned. "It makes sense. I've not been bothered by any night whisperings or bad thoughts, and the castle feels like a different place. It must have been her."

"Which means one problem solved but another created," I said. "What would you do to keep your treasure safe?"

"Anything! My treasure is precious to me." Lex tugged on his bottom lip. "I need to find a new hiding place. It must be protected. Just as jinn must grant wishes when we've been stimulated to do so, we must guard what's ours."

"I'm still thinking on those wishes," Wiggles said. "So far, it's all food related. I need to diversify my wish portfolio."

"Focus on our immediate mystery for now," I said to Lex. "You knew Florentine wanted your treasure while she was alive. Did you discover she'd returned and was after it again? Is that why you killed her for real this time?"

"Killed her?" His bottom lip wobbled as his face paled. "Tempest, I didn't kill her. Not the first time and not this time. I was certain she was dead."

"Which is impossible since she came here to steal from you."

He swallowed. "I engaged your services to solve this problem for me, not cause another one."

"Look at it from my point of view. You have a lousy alibi, you lied to me, and you would have done anything to make sure your wife couldn't get your treasure."

He stood and paced the room. "I understand this looks bad, but I didn't do it. I won't deny that when Florentine died, the first time, it was something of a relief. Of course, I was sad to lose my partner, but she'd become belligerent about the treasure, and her obsession for wasting what little she had was damaging. Jinn hoard treasures; we don't spend our treasures on material things."

"Florentine liked to splurge?"

"She became enamored by material objects." He raked a hand through his hair as he continued to pace. "She wanted more clothing and jewels she could wear and shoes. So many pairs of shoes. Her ways were deviant, and she was getting a bad reputation."

"You decided to get rid of an embarrassing problem?" I asked.

He rubbed the back of his neck. "Not by killing her. Not long before she died, I really wasn't sure she loved me at all. This confirms it. She was only with me because she wanted my treasure."

"Lex, she was a jinn! Just like you. You know exactly what it's like to be within touching distance of treasure you desire."

"It can make things... stressful. But she was also my wife," he said. "I thought I could change her and show her how jinn should behave."

"The way you're talking, it really suggests you had something to do with her death," I said, "either the first time or this time around."

"I didn't," he said. "I was on a different continent when she died in that landslide."

"The landslide didn't kill her," I said. "Florentine's been around this whole time. She was just waiting for you to make a mistake."

"And what a mistake I made," he said with a sigh. "My treasure has been revealed. Not only to Florentine but also to you."

"I want nothing to do with it," I said. "Don't even think about killing me as well to keep your secret."

He stared at me. "I wouldn't do that."

"I wouldn't mind a few pieces of your treasure," Wiggles said. "Although, with my three wishes waiting for me, I'll soon have everything I need."

"Quit it with the wish obsession," I said.

Lex strode over and grabbed my hand. "Tempest, I asked you to be my consultant because I want to prove my innocence. I want to know what happened with Florentine. You've already solved one mystery, but now you have to ensure I'm not seen as the guilty party."

I pulled my hand out of his grip. "Sorry to say you look guilty. Just because I'm helping with this investigation, it doesn't mean I'll hide the truth, even if the truth is that you did it."

"I didn't!" He stepped back, his face gray.

I wasn't convinced. Lex had everything going against him.

"I'm ready to ask for my first wish." Wiggles cleared his throat.

"Then you may proceed." Lex turned his attention to Wiggles, his face settling into a blank expression.

"My first wish is—"

I clamped my hand over Wiggles' mouth. "Hold it right there. You can have your wishes later. We need to leave."

Wiggles huffed on my hand and glared at me.

"What are you going to do?" Lex followed me to the door.

"Wiggles needs to think carefully about his wishes, and I'm going to speak to the angels."

"Please don't reveal my treasure to them," Lex said.

"It's not the treasure they'll be interested in." I headed out the front door.

"Tempest! Please! I'm innocent."

I shook my head. Lex looked guilty. He had a perfect motive, and he'd had the opportunity. Plus, he'd been the one to see the glowing figure in the grounds. Had he set this whole thing up?

Was Dazielle right all along? Was it always the husband that did it?

# Chapter 14

I wiped my palms on the back of my jeans as I strode beside Dazielle. We were walking toward the imposing high gate of the Darkwater maximum security prison.

She'd stuck to her word and arranged for me to visit Foxglove the day after my discovery of Lex's treasure in the castle.

I could have done with Wiggles by my side for this, but there was a rule about no animals in the prison. No matter how much he'd complained, I'd had to leave him behind. Although, I'd made him promise not to use any of his wishes in my absence. I wouldn't be happy if I returned to the apartment and found a dozen cute dogs, a pile of doughnuts, and Wiggles' new belly rub assistant sitting on the couch.

"Has Lex told you anything else useful?" After I'd spoken to Dazielle yesterday about Lex, they'd taken him into the station for questioning. He'd been there ever since.

"He seems defeated," Dazielle said. "From everything you've told me, he must have killed Florentine. He had everything to gain by getting rid of her. Jinn are weirdly possessive of their treasure. It's not the first time one has killed to protect what he thought he owned. I've put several behind bars for injuring someone who took a look at their gold without their permission."

"Lex did a good job of fooling me he was innocent," I said.

"Is that so difficult?" Dazielle smirked. "He had us all fooled with his charming ways and his luxurious castle. Now we know there's more to him than meets the eye, we can keep him for as long as we need while we get answers. It's only a matter of time before he lets something slip and implicates himself."

"What about the exhumation of Florentine's body?" I asked. "Has that given you any clues?"

"It wasn't her," Dazielle said. "Whoever the woman was that died in that landslide, it wasn't Florentine."

"Did Lex deliberately identify the wrong body, or was it a mistake?" I asked. "He wasn't happy in his marriage, so maybe he saw it as a way to get out. Declare your wife dead and move on."

"It's hard to know for certain, although he's still swearing it was Florentine. She'd been in the ground for two years, so I can't determine just how similar they looked, but they were the same height and had the same hair color."

"Florentine had to be behind faking her death," I said. "Otherwise, if Lex declared her dead, she could have simply popped up and said, hi, everyone, actually, I'm alive. What's this nonsense about me dying in a landslide? She set this up to make Lex think she was dead then waited to find his treasure."

"We'll get the truth out of Lex soon enough," Dazielle said. "This case is as good as closed. Once he cracks, and we get a confession, that'll be it."

"Then my work with Lex is over," I said. "And I doubt he'll want to compensate me for my time now he's in the frame for murdering Florentine."

Dazielle slowed before we reached the main gate of the prison. "Don't expect too much out of this visit."

"I just want the truth," I said. "I'm not expecting a warm welcome from Foxglove."

"What I mean is be skeptical of everything she tells you. Foxglove has a lot of time on her hands, and she might think it's amusing to mess with you."

"I'm prepared for her," I said. Although, my nerves were tingling with anticipation.

"Do you want me to come in with you?"

"No, she might not talk if there's an angel present. I need to do this on my own."

Dazielle briefly patted my arm. "I hope you find what you're looking for."

"So do I." My pulse raced as the gate in front of us slowly opened. Two large, brown-skinned ogres stood on either side.

"We have an appointment to see Foxglove Shadowsoul." Dazielle presented her credentials.

"This way." One of the ogres turned and walked beside a barrier with high wire mesh walls on either side.

I didn't need to get anywhere near the walls to feel the powerful magic wards keeping everything inside. If you ran into these walls during an escape, it would be your first and last attempt to get away.

We reached a set of doors and walked through into a beige reception area. We were met by a small, hook-nosed witch with a large stick dangling from her belt.

"I'm Warden Vossen. Put your belongings in the locker behind you," she said. "You can't take anything in when you're seeing the prisoner."

My keys and wallet went into the locker, along with my jacket.

"Are you carrying any spells, potions, hexes, enchanted objects, or curses?" she asked.

"Not today."

"Spread your arms and legs while I search you," Warden Vossen said.

"What are you looking for?" I lifted my arms.

"Contraband," she said. "It's amazing what people try to sneak in for prisoners. I've extracted vials of potions from places I really never want to see again."

I grimaced. "I'm hiding nothing."

Warden Vossen frisked me before waving a wand from my head down to my toes. "You're a witch plus... what else are you? I'm getting an odd reading."

"You're probably sensing Frank," I said. "I have a demon living inside me."

Her eyebrows flicked up. "Then you'll need double restraining magic. Witch and demon."

Dazielle leaned toward me. "Your magic will essentially be dampened when you visit. It means you can't harm the prisoners. Foxglove will be exactly the same. She won't be able to touch you with magic. They'll probably also have her in chains."

"Good to know," I said.

"Hold still while I do the spell," Warden Vossen said.

Her magic tingled from the top of my head over my arms and into my chest. For a second, it felt like I was trying to breathe underwater, then the magic continued down the rest of my body, and the air felt better.

Heaviness filled my limbs, and my brain grew foggy. "Am I supposed to feel so strange?"

"It's because you've got a double hit," Warden Vossen said. "Give it a few minutes; you'll get used to it. When you're ready, go through the door in front of you. The prisoner will be brought in. You've got five minutes."

"Why such a short amount of time?" I asked.

"Any longer, and she starts getting difficult. Foxglove is kept in a containment room most of the time. We've had a few... issues with her. That's all the time I can risk you being exposed to her."

That would have to be enough. I nodded at Dazielle before heading toward the door. I inched it open and entered a gray, featureless room set up with half a dozen benches. I sat at one and rested my hands on the top. I could already feel the magic settling into my system as my head cleared.

My nerves jumped with every noise coming from outside the room. I had to get this right and make Foxglove tell me what she knew about my dad.

The air pulsed with more magic. The wards around this room felt alive and powerful. They had to be. This place kept some seriously dark magic users under lock and key.

A door in front of me opened. Another large ogre stepped in and stood to one side, not acknowledging me.

A moment later, the door opened again. Foxglove walked in. She was dressed head to toe in black, her hair scraped off her face and magic shackles bound around her wrists.

Her eyes sparkled as she walked over.

Another ogre guard followed her and waited until she was in her seat before returning to the door.

"This is a treat," Foxglove said. "I'd hug you, but these restraints rather restrict my movement."

"I imagine they do," I said. "Settling in okay?"

"It already feels like a second home," she said. "Not that I plan on being here for long."

"You'll be here for as long as you have to be," I said, "which I'm pretty sure will be the rest of your life."

A scowl marred her face for a second before it was replaced with a smug smile. "I knew you wouldn't be able to stay away."

"Is that why you lied to me about my dad?"

"Was it a lie?" She grinned. "Would you be here if you didn't think there was truth in my words?"

I glared at her. "So, what do you know?"

"Come now, Tempest. Surely, you've been looking into what I told you," she said. "That was months ago. You haven't found him yet?"

"Maybe there's nothing to find. Tell me everything you know."

She tutted, but the sparkle in her eyes suggested she was getting a perverse pleasure out of this. "Why do you think he left?"

"I have no idea," I said. "I was a kid when he walked away."

"Perhaps he didn't feel appreciated." She inspected her short fingernails. "His life with you and your family must have been tedious. Will you be disappointed if you discover he's made a new, better life for himself? He might even have had more children. Imagine that, you have a half sister or brother out there somewhere. Would you like that?"

"Not particularly," I growled out. "And he did like his life with us. It wasn't tedious. I know he loved us. He didn't leave because of that."

"Perhaps he left because your mom was unfaithful."

My fingers flexed, and I leaned closer.

An ogre guard cleared his throat and shook his head at me.

I moved back in my seat. "Neither of them cheated."

"As you said, you were a child at the time. You probably missed half of what was going on between them."

"I wouldn't have missed that," I said. "Try again."

"They may simply have had nothing in common with each other," she said. "It happens. Couples grow apart. Eyes start to wander."

I slammed a hand on the table. "Stop jerking me around. I know he's been seen in the dark realm. What's he doing there?"

Her lips curled into a sly smile. "So, you have been doing your research. What else did you discover about him?"

"Dad was last seen six months ago," I said. "Why do you think he's hiding in the dark realm?"

"You must know that anyone who enters the dark realm is doing so to protect themselves. Your father must need a place to lie low because he's done something he's not proud of."

"What's he protecting himself from?"

"His tedious family?" She laughed softly. "You should go spend some time there. You might enjoy yourself."

Anger rolled over me, and sweat broke out on my brow. Frank was restless, and I sensed him trying to make his presence felt, but with the magic suppressing him, all he was able to do was make me overheat and feel even more frustrated.

"Having a little trouble?" Foxglove asked. "You get used to it after you've been here a while. I barely miss my powers."

Taking a deep breath, I fought to get my temper under control. "I've wasted my time coming here. You know nothing about my dad."

"I know more than you do," she said.

"Then tell me everything," I said. "What have you got to gain by keeping this information from me?"

"The satisfaction that I'm annoying you," she said. "After all, you put me in here."

"You put yourself in here," I said.

She looked around the room and sighed. "Axel hasn't been to visit yet. I've sent him several messages. Do you think he's avoiding me?"

"I can guarantee it. And are you surprised he hasn't come to see you? You told him you wanted him dead."

She tutted. "I said those words in the heat of the moment. He knows I didn't mean them. I always used to tease Axel about killing him when we were younger. It was a fun thing we'd do. Tell him to come see me."

"If I do that, will you tell me what you know about my dad?"

"We can come to some arrangement," she said. "But I want more than you simply passing on a message."

"What else do you want?"

She rested her hands flat on the table. "I don't suppose you want to come up with a plan to break me out of here? It could be fun getting one over on those ogres."

"There's not a chance of that happening," I said.

She shrugged. "I figured as much. I'll wait for my father to do that. He would never abandon me, not like some fathers we know."

It took all my self-control not to choke her. "It'll take more than Kroni's power to break through a place like this. You're stuck."

Her bottom lip jutted out. "He won't forsake me. If you won't break me out, then I want privileges."

"What kind of privileges?"

"The food in here is bad." Her chin dipped. "And they have no chocolate."

A bark of laughter came out of me. "You want me to send you chocolate?"

"I know you have a sweet tooth," she said. "Or rather, your demon does. It's the worst kind of torture not being able to indulge."

I nodded slowly. "I'll see what I can do on the chocolate front."

"Give me your word you'll send me some," she said.

"You have it," I said.

"And none of the cheap stuff," Foxglove said. "I want a high percentage of cocoa in every bar. Too much sugar and I get a headache."

"Now you're being picky." I sucked in a breath. "So, what do you know?"

She shifted in her seat as if getting comfortable. "Very well, I'll tell you. Your dad left to keep you and Aurora safe."

"Safe from what?"

"Take a guess." Her gaze ran over me.

"I don't get it. He was protecting us from something?"

Foxglove lifted her gaze to the ceiling. "He was protecting everyone from your demon."

My mouth dropped open. "He left because of Frank?"

A sneer crossed her face. "You don't really believe you have control over Frank, do you?"

"I do. We have an arrangement."

"No! You only think that. You were just a kid when you captured Frank. No child can hold a demon."

Doubt shifted through me, and my stomach tightened. Had Dad really done a deal with Frank?

Everyone had been stunned when I'd been able to contain the demon, but after a while, it just became the norm. Maybe it was only normal because of what Dad had done.

"How do you know this?" I asked.

"My source isn't important," she said. "I simply heard that your dad made a deal with Frank. He got a year to stay with the family before he had to leave and do Frank's bidding."

I sat back in my seat, my nerves fluttering and a sickness filling me with a dense dread. Those dates fit. Dad left one year after I'd stopped Aurora from being killed by Frank.

"I need proof," I said. "You could be making this up."

"I can't help with that," Foxglove said. "You'll have to take me on my word."

"That's not good enough."

"Then talk to Frank," she said. "He's your pet demon, after all. He'll tell you what deal he made with your father. It was bound in magic, I believe. A deal was done so Frank would let you live and not be a burden on your family. In return, your dad would leave and work for him."

"But Frank's a serious burden," I said. "He's come close to killing Aurora numerous times. He hasn't stuck to his end of the bargain."

"I suspect you've experienced Frank operating at half-strength," she said. "If he really wanted to get his claws into your sister, he'd do it."

The two guards made a move toward the table, and one pointed to the clock on the wall.

"Our time's up. Is there anything else you haven't told me?" I asked.

Foxglove stood and shook her head. "That's all you're getting. The rest is up to you. You know where your father was last seen, and you know why he left. Do you really want to get him back, knowing that would break the deal he has with Frank?"

"I don't know for certain a deal was ever made." My heart thudded at the worrying possibility Foxglove was right.

"It would be the end of you, your sister, and probably the rest of your family as they tried to defend themselves when Frank finally got loose. Do you want that on your conscience?"

"Time to move," a guard said as they both flanked Foxglove.

"Happy to oblige, handsome. Don't forget my chocolate," she said before turning and walking away.

I didn't move for several minutes. Was any of that true? Had my dad left after making a deal with Frank, so I'd stay safe and be able to control him?

My eyes grew hot, and I blinked quickly. I felt cheated. How had Dad known I wouldn't have been able to handle Frank?

I sighed. Because Dad was the wise one. He'd always had such a level head and sensible words whenever anyone needed them. And this was just the sort of thing he'd do to protect his family.

My knees shook as I headed back to Dazielle. I had to speak to my dad. I needed to find him and discover if any of this was true.

And if it was, what then? I still wanted him back, but if I found him, would that mean Frank broke free and my whole family would be in danger?

I walked to the waiting area where Dazielle sat. I collected my things, and we left the prison together.

"How did it go?" she asked. "Did you get the answers you need?"

I stared into the distance, not paying attention to what I was seeing. "I got more questions than answers."

She opened her mouth as if to ask more but then simply held out her hand. "Let's get out of here. We'll magic back to the village to save time, unless you want to fly back with me."

I grimaced. "Magic's fine."

My stomach flipped as the translocation spell took effect, and we arrived outside the doors of Angel Force.

"What are you going to do now?" Dazielle asked.

I stumbled away. "Fix this mess once and for all." The trouble was, I didn't know how.

I needed time alone to think and work out exactly what to do with this new information.

# Chapter 15

I'd been wandering around the stone circle for half an hour, my thoughts refusing to settle and form an orderly plan, when I spotted Wiggles bounding toward me.

He always found me. Anytime I left Willow Tree Falls, the moment I stepped back into the village, he'd sniff me out.

He padded over toward me. "You didn't come home. What happened at the prison?"

I ran my fingers over the rough surface of one of the stones in the circle. They all thrummed with an ancient, reassuring magic. "Foxglove told me my dad left because of me. She said he made a deal with Frank. He wouldn't destroy me or the family, and in return, Dad would work for Frank."

"Huh! I'd have never figured that out." Wiggles trotted along beside me. "You think she's telling the truth?"

"I can find out if she's lying," I said. "I know where Dad was last seen. And I can always ask Frank."

"Foxglove's messing with you," he said. "She's doing this, so you'll doubt yourself."

I sighed and tipped my head back. "It's working. Do you remember that first year after I'd captured Frank? It was hard. I always assumed it was because I was young and hadn't come into my full powers. What if it had nothing to do with that?"

"You think your dad saw you struggling and somehow communicated with Frank? He struck a deal to keep you safe?"

I nodded. "I used to find myself in Aurora's bedroom at least once a week. Frank used to sleepwalk me there, so he could look at her."

"I remember," Wiggles said. "I used to follow you, sometimes."

"I also remember taking weapons in with me. One time, I woke and had a baseball bat in my hands. I wanted to hit her. And Aurora woke up one night to find me holding a pillow over her head. That was Frank. Maybe he was testing the boundaries and warning my dad what would happen if he didn't hold up his end of the bargain."

"Or maybe it was you adjusting to your new guest," Wiggles said.

"No, it's all falling into place," I said. "After Dad left, Frank was more manageable. He still had his moments, but he wasn't being so difficult. That has to be connected. Foxglove's telling the truth. Dad left to keep me safe."

"You can keep yourself safe now," Wiggles said. "You're more powerful than Frank."

I rubbed my fingers through his fur as I ducked beside him. "Not all the time. Sometimes, he beats me."

"But not for long. You always get back control." He flipped on his side, so I could rub his belly.

"You're right. I do. And he's not going to beat me now. Frank, we need to talk." I dropped a few barriers and waited for him to emerge.

Nothing stirred.

I dropped another barrier. "There's no use hiding. You must have heard my conversation with Foxglove. What can you tell me about the deal you made with my dad?"

Frank still refused to stir.

"What's he saying?" Wiggles asked.

"He's silent. That's never a good sign. It usually means he's hiding something." I cautiously dropped another barrier. "Frank, what do you know about my dad leaving? Did you have something to do with it? Do you know where he is now?"

He still wasn't budging.

I dropped my final barrier. He could easily come through and take complete control. There was nothing stopping him.

He didn't even sigh. I felt nothing. That only confirmed my worst fears. Frank was behind my dad leaving, and he realized I'd be more than a little annoyed with him now I'd discovered this.

My head shot up as screams echoed through the forest. I slammed my barriers back into place before stepping outside the stone circle and staring into the trees.

A pale-skinned woman with long flaxen hair dashed out of the forest. She was running so fast her movements were a blur. As she ran, smoke trailed behind her. Her hair was on fire!

"Leave this place, foul demon." Fallon raced out of the forest, a blazing arrow notched in her bow as she chased after the woman, who, from her unnaturally stunning looks, must be a vampire.

"Stop!" Suki thundered out of the forest, her cheeks bright red as she tried to catch Fallon.

The woman caught my gaze and diverted toward the stone circle, still being pursued by Fallon and Suki.

"Help me!" she gasped. "That forest creature is insane." She almost fell into my arms. Up close, she was so beautiful it hurt my eyes to look at her. Her skin was flawless, and she had a cute upturned nose that went perfectly with her full mouth.

"Let's get these flames out. I'm going to have to roll you." I dropped her to the ground and spun her in the dirt a few times until the flames were gone.

I held my hand out and helped her up before patting her back to get the final flickers of flame. "What were you doing in the forest to upset Fallon?"

"Nothing! I didn't know the forest was out of bounds." She looked over her shoulder and glared at Fallon, who was still approaching with a fiery arrow.

"It isn't," I said. "But Fallon's protective of the forest. She can be overzealous when she meets somebody she doesn't know."

"More like crazy," the woman said. "Thanks for helping me. I'm Nisha Naparo."

"Tempest Crypt," I said.

"You captured the enemy." Fallon leaped into the stone circle and raised her arrow.

I held up a hand. "Stop! What are you doing?"

"That creature was in my forest." Fallon's dark eyes narrowed.

"Doing what?"

"Walking around like she owned the place."

Suki puffed up behind her and knocked the bow out of Fallon's hand. "I'm so sorry about this. This isn't what a forest guardian's supposed to do."

"Hey! That's my favorite bow." Fallon bent and picked up the weapon before glaring at Suki. "How are we supposed to fell this night creature if you break my bow?"

"Maybe you're not going to fell anyone," I said. "Did you ask her what she was doing in the forest, other than walking around?"

"I follow my gut on these matters." Fallon lifted her chin. "My gut told me not to trust her."

"That's most likely trapped wind talking," Wiggles muttered.

"Fallon, that's enough," Suki said, her voice full of warning. "How many times do we have to talk about this? You need to question people in the forest before you try to kill them."

"Kill me!" Nisha backed away. "I don't deserve that."

"Oh, no! I'm sure you don't." Suki held up a hand. "We don't kill many people who come into the forest."

"Speak for yourself," Fallon said.

Now everyone was out of the immediate threat of death from Fallon's overenthusiastic killing urges, I turned to Nisha. "I don't recognize you from around here. Are you visiting someone in Willow Tree Falls?"

She kept her gaze on Fallon. "That's right. I have a friend in the village, another half-vampire."

"I don't believe that," Fallon said. "You were lurking with intent in my forest. I don't expect your friend lives there."

"The forest belongs to everyone," Suki said. "People are allowed to walk in it."

"But not lurk in it," Fallon said. "I've forbidden that."

"Were you lurking?" I asked Nisha.

"No! I was simply killing time."

"Who's your friend?" I asked.

"Brogan Costin. He runs Unicorn's Trough. Do you know him?"

I nodded. He'd never mentioned anyone called Nisha, but I didn't know all his friends. "Why were you waiting for him in the forest?"

"I was just exploring. He gets busy in the evenings, and I didn't want to get in his way while he was working. I meant no harm by being here. I certainly didn't expect to get set on fire by some crazed wood nymph."

I glanced at Fallon, but from the stubborn set of her jaw, she had no intention of apologizing.

"Have you known Brogan long?" I asked.

"Years," she said. "We used to date, and we've been in touch again recently. He suggested I stop by some time. I decided to surprise him."

"I expect he'll be happy to see you," I said.

"I doubt that. Never trust a lurker; that's what I say. She's only causing problems for herself," Fallon said.

Nisha glared at her. "You're the one causing problems. Brogan will be mad when he finds out you were hunting me."

"Was it ever serious between you and Brogan?" I asked Nisha.

She leaned closer to me. "Of course! He's such a flirt, but I could tell he was interested the last time we spoke. There's a chance we might get back together. I'm recently single."

"He could do with a friend right now," I said.

"Why's that?" she asked.

"He's recently lost someone he was close to," I said.

Color flared across Nisha's cheeks. "I didn't know that. What kind of friend? A girl?"

From the jealous glint in her eyes, Nisha had a possessive side. "A female friend. They were close."

She snorted a derisive laugh. "I'm sure it wasn't serious."

"You'll have to check that with Brogan," I said, "but it sounded serious to me."

She backed away, shaking her head. "You're mistaken. Who is this woman?"

My eyes narrowed. Nisha had jealous ex-girlfriend stamped all over her. And jealous people could be dangerous. "How long have you been in Willow Tree Falls?"

"Just a day. Why do you ask?"

"I'm curious," I said.

"You don't trust this one either," Fallon said. "You see, gut instinct. It never fails me. Shall I shoot her now?"

I turned to Fallon. "No shooting, not just yet."

Fallon grumbled as she lowered the bow. "How am I supposed to protect the forest if I'm not allowed to use my weapons?"

"You're crazy," Nisha muttered. "I should report you to the angels. I'm getting out of here." She turned and hurried away.

I watched her go. Brogan would have his hands full with that one, but maybe she was just what he needed. A flirty distraction after Florentine's death.

That reminded me I still hadn't spoken to him about his involvement with Florentine, not that it mattered now. Lex was in custody, and it was only a matter of time before he confessed and was charged with her murder.

"I need to get back to the forest," Fallon said. "Give me a ride, pony."

"No." Wiggles sat and bared his teeth at Fallon.

"Huh! Bad pony. You need more training." She turned and strode away.

Suki shot me an apologetic look. "I've extended her probation period as forest guardian. She'll get there in the end. She's so enthusiastic about the protection side of things. I'll see you later at the club." She raised a hand before hurrying after Fallon.

I slumped against a stone and closed my eyes. I couldn't think about anything other than my dad and what my next move needed to be.

Frank wasn't talking, but maybe someone in my family knew more about this.

I pushed away from the stone. "Come on, Wiggles. Let's go home."

"Any chance of some pizza?"

"Why not?"

"Excellent. Pizza makes everything better. I also recommend garlic bread, curly fries, and milkshakes. And then we can talk about my wishes."

Maybe pizza would make things better tonight, but tomorrow, I had people to speak to. I would keep asking questions about Dad until I got a definitive answer.

Even if it wasn't the one I wanted to hear.

# Chapter 16

I'd had a restless night, thinking about Dad. The one thing I knew for certain was that I had to see him. If he was still alive, I had to make contact. Things were different now. I had my full powers and was able to control Frank, most of the time. Dad could forget about the deal he'd made and return home. He could come back to his family, where he belonged.

After my shower, I stood in front of the bathroom mirror and stared at my reflection. "Why don't you want to talk, Frank? Are you afraid of what'll happen to you now I've discovered the truth?"

He was still operating in silent mode. No matter what I did, I couldn't get him to respond.

"How about a long weekend out of Willow Tree Falls, and you can do anything you like?"

I still got no response.

"A no holds-barred weekend of fun. No repercussions for you. This is a one-time deal. I won't offer it again." I wasn't sure I would let Frank out unrestrained. He'd cause carnage, but I'd do just about anything to get him to tell me what he knew.

"We could go on a gourmet, all-inclusive cruise. You could eat whatever you like and try all the different desserts of the world, one after another. Wouldn't you like that?"

He didn't answer.

"Frank! You'll speak to me, eventually. You can't stay hidden forever. I know you're there, and you know something about this."

I shook my head when he didn't answer. I dressed quickly and dried my hair before grabbing a quick breakfast with Wiggles and then heading out of the apartment.

"Where are we going?" he asked.

"Someone in this family must know what happened between Frank and Dad."

"You're thinking Granny Dottie might have some answers?" Wiggles asked. "She knows something about everything."

"She's the perfect place to start," I said. "She has all the best gossip. Maybe Dad confided in her about what he'd planned to do. Granny Dottie may even have helped him. I have no memory of Dad ever talking directly to Frank, but he could have done it while I was asleep or under the influence of a spell."

"Hey! Tempest."

I turned and saw Brogan striding toward me. Dark circles marred his normally handsome face. It looked like he hadn't slept in days.

"Brogan, I can't stop. I'm sort of busy right now. Family business."

He raked a hand through his hair as he stopped in front of me and blocked my path. "I've been trying to find you. I keep hearing all these rumors about Flossie."

"You mean Florentine?"

He sighed. "Yes, my girlfriend and Lex's wife."

"Everything's getting sorted," I said. "Lex is being questioned over what happened to her."

His nostrils flared, and he flashed his fangs. "Lex killed her? Has he confessed?"

"Not yet," I said. "But he's got a great motive and a lousy alibi. It turns out that whoever he buried two years ago wasn't his wife. I reckon Florentine faked her own death."

He shook his head. "Why would she do that?"

I side-stepped Brogan. I needed to go. "You should ask the angels."

He caught hold of my arm. "I'm asking you."

I gritted my teeth. "Lex was lying to her. He was hiding his treasure, and she wanted it. Florentine waited until he moved into the castle and then set to work on sending him crazy, so she could get her hands on it. Lex must have found out and decided to silence her to protect his treasure."

A growl rumbled in Brogan's chest. "That doesn't sound like the woman I knew. Flossie was sweet and kind. She was funny." His voice cracked. "She was so beautiful."

"I wish I could help," I said, "but I really have to get on."

He dragged a hand down his face, his body radiating defeat. "It makes no sense. I don't know what to do."

"You'll figure things out." I took a step away but stopped. Brogan looked broken. As much as I wanted to figure out the mystery surrounding my dad, I couldn't leave him like this. "Come on. Let's go to the café. I could do with one of your amazing coffees."

"I haven't even opened today," he said. "I haven't felt like doing anything since I learned what happened to Flossie."

"Then we've got time to talk if you don't have customers to serve." I nudged him in the direction of Unicorn's Trough.

He scraped his feet along the ground as he walked, his head down.

I waited with Wiggles as he unlocked the door, and we walked in behind him. He kept the sign turned to closed and the blinds down before heading around the counter and switching on the coffee machine.

"Do you want anything to eat?" he asked.

"I'll have some muffins," Wiggles said. "And if you've got any waffles, that would be good. Maybe a side order of bear claw?"

"Enough," I muttered.

Brogan grunted a laugh. "Take a seat. I'll bring it all over. Anything for you, Tempest?"

"I wouldn't mind a muffin."

"Coming right up."

I settled in my seat, and Wiggles sat by my feet.

"He doesn't look too good," he muttered.

I nodded. Brogan was my friend, and even though I had my own problems to deal with, I couldn't walk away after seeing him in such a mess.

Brogan walked over and set down a tray of pastries, muffins, and two large mugs of coffee.

I took a muffin and passed Wiggles a bear claw, which he set about with noisy delight. "You're not having anything?" I asked Brogan.

"I can't handle eating right now," he said. "My grandparents took me out to hunt last night, but I wasn't in the mood for anything fresh. Nothing they offered tempted me. Ever since I lost Flossie, I mean, Florentine, I can't find much meaning in my life anymore."

"You fell for her hard by the sound of it," I said. "How long were you dating?"

"Three months," he said. "She showed up one day in the café and completely charmed me."

"Three months, you say?" I tilted my head. "Around the time Lex bought the castle?"

He tipped back in his seat and groaned. "I didn't even think about that, but you're right."

"I think Florentine was watching her husband. She saw an opportunity when he bought Castle Falls. She knew he'd move his treasure hoard there."

He was quiet for a moment. "That's what she really wanted?"

"I reckon so."

"And Flossie decided to entertain herself with me while waiting for her chance to get the treasure." Brogan snarled and glared out the window. "I was so easily fooled. She seemed so honest. She even told me she'd been married."

"Did she say what happened to her husband?" I bit into my chocolate muffin.

"Not much, but she left the marriage because he mistreated her."

"And you believed that?"

He rubbed his forehead with the tips of his fingers before sipping his coffee. "I don't know what to believe anymore. I got no hint Flossie was being dishonest. Maybe their marriage was an unhappy one. She could have left to start again."

"Lex admitted things weren't great between them before she died, the first time," I said. "He felt relieved she was gone."

"You don't think he had anything to do with the first attempt on her life?" Brogan asked.

"You think Lex caused a landslide?"

"I know it seems unlikely," he said.

"Florentine most likely faked her death," I said. "Things between her and Lex were strained, and she was getting desperate. She figured out he'd never reveal where his treasure was, so she needed another way to discover it. She was prepared to wait to get her hands on such a hoard. And trust me, I've seen only a fraction of it, but Lex has an enormous amount of treasure in that castle. What's a couple of years of waiting when you know that's coming into your possession eventually?"

"Florentine was watching her husband, waiting for a chance to steal from him?" His shoulders slumped. "I've been such an idiot."

"No, you haven't. You got your head turned by a beautiful woman. There's nothing wrong with that. And don't worry. The angels are on top of things for once. They believe Lex is her killer. Florentine's death won't go unpunished."

"And you're sure he did it?" Brogan's stare was intense. "I've met Lex several times. I thought he was a good guy. Never had him down as someone shady."

I'd barely thought about anything other than my dad these past twenty-four hours. I took a moment to shift through the suspects. "Honestly, out of all the people it might have been, I wouldn't have picked Lex Fontaine. But with his terrible alibi and a really great motive, he fits. Jinns are super possessive of their treasure."

Brogan lowered his head. "I've never said this to anyone, but I loved Florentine. She must have realized that. Why ruin what we had?"

"Treasure trumps anything when it comes to jinn." I patted the back of his hand. "Try not to take it personally. Maybe she really did like you. Right guy, wrong time."

He grunted as he lifted his head. "Yeah. So much that she was also dating that guy working at the castle."

I winced. "You've heard about her relationship with Gregor?" I'd deliberately not revealed who else Florentine had been seeing in case Brogan decided to hunt him down.

"Sure. Everyone who's come in the cafe wants to share the gossip. It took all my self-control and Grandad's warning not to find Gregor and punch his lights out." Brogan sighed. "It wasn't his fault, though. Flossie, or whatever her name was, she tricked us all."

"Maybe she couldn't resist your charms," I said. "You have a lot to offer a girl."

"Nice try, Tempest." He shook his head. "I should have known better. She was just out to have a bit of fun. I keep my distance when it comes to relationships for just this reason. You let your guard down, and someone gets in and hurts you."

"You'll find someone a hundred times better," I said. "She wasn't the right one for you."

"Yeah. I guess I haven't yet met the right one," he said. "It's a shame you're dating Rhett. You get me. We could be good together."

I grinned. "I guess I do. But I'm happy with Rhett. How about your old girlfriend, Nisha? Maybe she can comfort you while she's around."

His eyes widened. "Nisha? How do you know her?"

"I saw her yesterday at the stone circle," I said. "Hasn't she been in to see you yet? She was waiting for the dinner crowd to quieten before she came by."

He shoved back his seat and stood. "Please tell me this is some sick joke."

I glanced at Wiggles, who looked as puzzled as I felt. "No joke. She was chased out of the forest by Fallon. Don't you two get along anymore?"

He paced the café as he raked his hands through his hair. "No! She can't be here. This is a nightmare."

"Did you have a bad breakup?"

"You could say that. She's insane and dangerous." He pulled down his T-shirt to expose his chest. "And the last time we argued, she tried to stake me through the heart."

# Chapter 17

I stared at the pale scar on Brogan's chest. "Nisha did that to you?"

He covered the scar and gave a swift nod. He walked to the table and sat opposite me. "I've known her five years. When I first met Nisha, she was funny and sweet and always happy to do whatever I suggested."

"Anything you suggested?" I arched an eyebrow.

He rolled his eyes. "Her true colors soon surfaced. I told her I only wanted a casual relationship right from the start. She said that wasn't a problem. She wasn't looking for anything serious. Turns out, the opposite was true."

"She wanted a ring on her finger?" I asked.

"You've got that right. I discovered a pile of magazines in her apartment all about weddings. She'd been planning our dream wedding and had conveniently forgotten to mention it to me. Of course, I called things to a halt right away."

I wrinkled my nose. "I get that seems weird to a lot of guys, but for some girls, it's their thing. They've dreamed about getting married since they were kids. It doesn't necessarily mean Nisha planned to marry you."

He snorted a laugh. "She tried the same line on me, but I showed her the picture I'd found. She'd cut off our heads and superimposed them on top of a bride and groom. That was it. I was out of there."

"I imagine she wasn't happy about that."

"Nisha was raging mad. She hassled me for weeks, trying to convince me it was a joke and I was taking it too seriously, but I saw the glint in her eyes," Brogan said. "She wanted marriage, and she wanted it with me."

"And you're not the marrying kind?"

He sagged in his seat. "I was beginning to change my mind after meeting Flossie, but I made a mistake. I won't get tricked again. I'd never marry Nisha. She's crazy jealous. At first, it was kinda cute. Then it got annoying."

"So, what happened to make Nisha try to kill you?"

"I thought she'd given up on trying to win me back," he said. "But about two years after the relationship ended, she showed up. She said she'd been doing a lot of soul searching and was making amends to anyone she'd wronged. She apologized for being so full on and not being honest about wanting a serious relationship. She seemed genuine, so I forgave her. We had a fun evening together and had a couple of drinks. Then she made a move on me. Everything she'd told me was false. It was just another trick to get me back. I set her straight. There was no chance for us."

"And she flipped out?"

"She went berserk. That's when she smashed a chair and tried to plunge the broken leg into my heart. A couple of inches deeper, and we wouldn't be having this conversation."

I sipped on my coffee and studied Brogan's face. "Now Nisha's in Willow Tree Falls at the same time the woman you were in love with gets killed." Was that a chance occurrence, or was there more to Nisha's visit than I'd first thought?

His eyes sparkled with anger, and his fangs appeared as his top lip curled up. "Do you think Nisha killed Flossie?"

I lifted a hand. "I've no proof, and most of the clues are leading to Lex, but your psycho ex-girlfriend comes to the village just as you're getting serious with somebody else. Then Florentine is killed."

A growl rumbled low in Brogan's chest, and he stood, kicking his chair away. "I will kill her."

"You'll have to find her first," I said. "Most likely, Fallon's already chased her out of the village. She set Nisha on fire for being in the forest. It was made very clear she wasn't welcome."

"That won't stop her. I'll hunt Nisha down and destroy her if she had anything to do with Flossie's murder." His fingers clenched into fists, and he slammed one down on the table, cracking the wood.

"Cool your heels for now," I said. "The angels are still looking at Lex, and we don't want anybody else dead."

Although, now I'd taken a few minutes to consider it, I was never completely sold on Lex killing Florentine. It was almost too neat. Too easy.

Brogan huffed out a long breath before running a hand down his face. "Whenever Nisha's around, things get intense. I wouldn't put murder past her."

"Maybe suggest to Dazielle that they speak to Nisha. If she's as possessive as you claim, she might be considered a suspect. When we spoke, she was dismissive of your relationship with Florentine. She's hopeful you'll get back together."

He shook his head. "Nisha sounds as deranged as ever. I haven't spoken to her in over two years. I cut all ties after she tried to kill me. She can't think I'd forgive her for that."

"How about I try to find her?" I said. "I can speak to her and learn where she was on the night of Florentine's murder. She might have a good alibi and can be ruled out."

Brogan scowled and glared out the window for several seconds before nodding. "Be careful around Nisha. She has a temper, and she's unstable. I bear a scar as evidence."

"I've got no plans to confront her on my own. But you need to keep your head down. She might come after you again to get revenge."

"I'll be ready for her if she does," he said. "She won't get anywhere near my heart this time."

I pushed my chair back and stood. "Just keep a low profile until I figure out where Nisha's hiding and what her plans are."

His eyes narrowed. "I'll take her out if she comes for me. I don't care that we used to date. If I find out she had anything to do with Flossie's murder, you won't be able to stop me from getting my revenge."

I patted his arm as I walked past. "Let's hope it doesn't come to that. I'll catch up with you later." I left Unicorn's Trough with Wiggles, my pace fast. If Brogan decided to act, I didn't have much time to find Nisha and get the truth out of her.

My shoulders ached with tension. I wanted to focus on finding my dad, but I had to put that on hold for a short while.

I needed to find Nisha. If she'd discovered Brogan was in a serious relationship and had gotten rid of the competition, she might be planning a strike against him. Her final act of revenge. If she couldn't have him, maybe Nisha wanted to make sure no one else could.

Brogan was my friend. I wouldn't let anything bad happen to him.

"Where to now?" Wiggles asked.

"Back to see your favorite forest guardian," I said.

He glowered up at me, and smoke drifted from his nose. "Do we have to?"

"She was one of the last people to see Nisha. Fallon could have useful information."

"She's also as unstable as Nisha," he said. "She has an unhealthy obsession with trying to kill people."

"Fallon does her slaying in the line of duty," I said. "But you're right. She does tend to shoot first and ask questions later."

We walked the short distance away from the stores and headed along the main trail path of the forest.

"Fallon's usually somewhere on the perimeter," I said. "Keep checking overhead. She likes to hide in the branches and watch people as they walk along this path."

We'd been walking for ten minutes before I slowed. The hairs on the back of my neck rose as a sensation of being watched hit me.

"I think we've—"

"Hi-yah! You're mine now, little pony." Fallon descended from a branch and landed on Wiggles' back.

He snapped and snarled as he bucked, trying to dislodge his unwelcome rider.

Fallon clung to his ears, squeaking with delight and slapping his haunch with her free hand. "Go faster!"

"Fallon!" I hurried after them, trying to grab her off Wiggles' back before he bit her or burned her alive. "Get off Wiggles! He hates being ridden."

"Yee-haw! This is the best ride I've had in ages." She wrapped an arm around Wiggles' neck and pressed her face on the top of his head. "Now charge, my trusty, furry steed."

"No charging!" I raced after them as Wiggles continued to buck and snarl. "Wiggles! Stay still for a second."

He growled, and a jet of fire spat from his mouth. "Get this crazed creature off me."

I finally caught hold of the back of Fallon's tunic collar and yanked her off.

Wiggles yipped and scurried away. "My ears! She's dislocated them."

I held Fallon up by her collar and glared at her. "Let's get one thing straight. Wiggles is my hellhound. I get to say who rides him."

"No one gets to ride me," he grumbled, flicking his ears backward and forward.

"You've never minded sharing him before." Fallon looked incredulous.

"I mind now. My hellhound, my rules."

Fallon kicked her legs in the air and scowled at me. "I'm not used to being treated in such a disrespectful way in my own forest."

I shook her by the collar. "And one more thing. This forest belongs to all of us. Everyone who lives in Willow Tree Falls has the right to walk in it without getting flaming arrows shot at them, stuck in poisonous webbing, or stuck down holes. You have to rein it in when it comes to protecting the forest."

Her eyes grew wide, and she stopped struggling. "I must protect it. The trees are sacred, and all the magic items hidden here must never be discovered. If the forest becomes damaged, that'll be my fault. I might be dismissed from my position."

"You'll be dismissed permanently when I get my teeth on you," Wiggles said. "I think I've got a pulled muscle in my ear."

Fallon grumbled under her breath and continued to glare at me. "Maybe we can make a deal about riding the pony."

"Here's the deal," I said. "No more uninvited rides. You might occasionally get a ride if it's an emergency and you need to get somewhere quickly, but you don't just leap on him whenever you want."

"I'm my own hellhound. I'll not be exploited." Wiggles lifted his nose in the air.

"Got that?" I said to Fallon. "No exploiting Wiggles."

"Then you must allow me to run the forest as I see fit," she said.

"That's not the deal," I said.

She huffed. "I only want to ride him so much because I love him."

I glanced at Wiggles and saw his eyes widen. "You love Wiggles?" I lowered her slowly to the ground.

"Of course I do. He's magnificent. Get past the stumpy legs, flatulence, and stench of sulfur, and he's perfect. If I could dream up my ideal riding steed, it would be him. I fell under his charms the first day we met. I make no apologies for wanting to ride him. When I'm on Wiggles' back, I feel like a different person. Carefree and happy. I don't have to worry about forest magic or evil doings in my woods."

I scratched my head. I hadn't expected that from Fallon. I figured she rode Wiggles because she knew how much he hated it and got a thrill out of annoying him.

Wiggles cleared his throat and took a step closer. "I'm your perfect steed? I mean, not that I'm a steed. But if I was, if you had every steed in the world available to you, I'd be the one you'd choose?"

Fallon held out a hand. She opened her palm to reveal a chocolate candy. "You absolutely are. I feel blessed that you've come into my life."

Wiggles nipped forward, grabbed the chocolate candy, and backed away as he ate it.

"Well, that's good of you to say, Fallon," I said. "But you have to respect Wiggles' wishes about the no riding bit."

"Maybe she can ride me now and again," he said swiftly, "once my ears have recovered. And so long as she feeds me candy."

Fallon clapped her hands together. "I can really ride you? Whenever I like?"

"Hold on," I said. "What are you saying? You hate being ridden."

"I am the perfect steed," Wiggles said. "Perfect steeds might be willing to give more regular rides."

I groaned and dropped my head into my hands. "You aren't even a pony."

"I can be whatever I want to be," Wiggles said. "A person is only hindered by their imagination."

"You absolutely can!" Fallon clapped her hands together again. "And if you want to be my perfect steed, then you must be."

I never thought I'd hear Wiggles support Fallon's desire to ride him. "Well, now that's all sorted. Fallon, we're looking for Nisha, the half-vampire you chased out of the forest yesterday. Have you seen her since then?"

Her eyes narrowed, and a scowl crossed her face. "That one's trouble. She's stealthy and quiet. It turns out, she's been in the forest for some time. She must have snuck past me in a moment of weakness."

"She's been staying in the forest?" I asked.

"That's right," Fallon said. "She was using a cave. I've been keeping watch on it in case she has the nerve to return and collect her things."

"Can you show us the cave?"

"Do I get to ride my pony?"

"Wiggles?" I asked.

"Just don't touch the ears," he said. "They're really sore after you grabbed them."

Fallon bounced onto his back and wrapped her arms around his neck before kissing his head. "I'll never hurt my little pony. Giddy up, we'll lead the way. Straight ahead."

I shook my head as the two most unlikely of companions continued to bond as Fallon discussed riding routes and what Wiggles' favorite candy was.

We'd been walking for fifteen minutes, when Fallon slowed Wiggles. "It's the cave up ahead. She concealed it well, but I could see things had been moved. That's where I found her bag."

I hurried ahead and pushed aside some branches placed across the entrance of the cave. A small bag was set to one side, which I picked up and emptied on the ground.

I picked up several photographs and a worn notebook. The pictures were all of Florentine, and the eyes had been scrubbed out by something sharp.

"That doesn't look good," Wiggles said as he looked at the photographs.

"It shows she hated Florentine," I said. "And she knew all about her relationship with Brogan."

"Why is that important?" Fallon asked.

"I'm not sure yet," I said. "But Nisha might be involved with what happened to Florentine Fontaine."

"I heard the angels had someone in custody for that," she said.

"They do. But maybe it's the wrong somebody." I flicked through the notepad. "No way!"

"Have you found a signed confession?" Wiggles asked.

"No, but it's almost as good. This looks like a journal written by Florentine." I kept reading. "Nisha must have gotten hold of it somehow."

"Don't keep us hanging." Wiggles nudged my calf.

I flicked through several pages, reading as fast as I could. "She's got records of when she saw Lex and what she did to him. This proves it was her all along. She was the demon, and she wanted to get rid of him to get the treasure. Oh! And here's something about Brogan and Gregor."

My head shot up at the sound of a branch snapping underfoot.

I pressed a finger to my lips before inching back to the cave entrance.

A surprised looking Nisha stared in the cave before she turned and bolted through the trees.

"Stop!" I raced out after her.

"We'll get her." Fallon raced past on Wiggles' back. "Take down the enemy. Let's destroy her."

"Don't destroy her just yet," I yelled as I tried to keep up. "I've got a few questions for Nisha."

Nisha's vampire speed meant there was no way we'd catch her on foot. I was just conjuring a spell when there was a shriek from up ahead.

I grimaced as I increased my pace. Fallon had probably attacked her with a flaming bow or speared her through the heart with a poisoned dart. I'd lost my chance to question her.

I slowed as I reached Fallon and Wiggles, who were peering into a hole in the ground.

Fallon glanced up and grinned. "We got her. I told you my traps were effective. I must dig more of these."

I looked into the hole. Glaring up at me was a red-faced Nisha.

"Get me out of here," she snapped.

"You're not going anywhere until you answer some questions," I said.

"I'm not telling you anything." She jumped and almost made it to the top of the hole, but her fingers grappled the edge before she fell.

She shrieked in frustration and tried several more times. Each time, she was just a couple of inches short.

"I'm always careful when I dig my traps." Fallon folded her arms over her chest, a look of intense satisfaction on her face. "Although these traps can't keep in creatures who fly, anything that needs to jump to get out will fail. I have a ninety-five percent success rate on my traps."

Nisha hissed angrily before she slumped against the mud wall. "I've done nothing wrong. You can't keep me here."

"What do you know about this woman?" I threw a picture of Florentine down to her.

Nisha looked at the picture. "I don't know her."

"That was in your bag," I said, "along with several others. I'm guessing you were the one who gouged out her eyes on that photo."

"What if I did?"

"Have you seen her recently?"

She shrugged. "Maybe I have. It's not important."

"And you knew she was involved with Brogan?"

Nisha stared silently at me.

"You're not getting out until you answer," Fallon said. She looked up at me. "Shall I bring my flaming arrows to encourage her to talk?"

"Not just yet," I said.

Nisha tapped her fingers on her arm before sighing. "No flaming arrows. I'll admit that I saw that cheating jinn with Brogan a few times."

"Brogan mentioned he hasn't seen you in over two years," I said.

She shrugged. "What if he hasn't? I still like to check up on him now and again."

"Psycho ex-girlfriend much?" Wiggles muttered.

Nisha glared at him. "I'm looking out for the man I love. Brogan can be careless with his affections. He also believes he's invincible and everyday rules don't apply to him. I don't know what he was thinking, getting mixed up with a deceitful jinn."

"He knows he's not invincible, especially after you tried to drive a wooden chair leg into his chest," I said.

Her mouth opened and closed several times. "How do you know about that?"

"He showed me the scar," I said.

"You've seen Brogan naked?" She growled at me. "Are you involved with him?"

"If I was, would you try to get rid of me?"

She snorted a laugh. "As if he'd be interested in a witch. I did that for his own good. Brogan sometimes forgets how important our relationship is. He gets his head turned by an attractive woman, and his obligations to me disappear."

"What obligations does he have to you?" I asked. "You had a casual relationship, which he broke off when he realized you wanted to get married."

She jabbed a finger at me. "Brogan wanted to marry me. He always told me so."

"Or did you only imagine that's what he wanted?" I said.

"He loves me. He's always loved me." She sniffed. "He just likes playing hard to get."

I held up the journal. "Where did you get this?"

"I found it," Nisha said.

"It's not yours," I said. "You took it from Florentine. Did you read it?"

"Some of it. It's full of lies. And it shows she was cheating on Brogan. He wouldn't want her."

"You were going to show him this?" I asked. "You thought, if he saw this, he'd get rid of Florentine and pick you?"

"Of course! That journal proves how wrong she was for him. Hounding her husband, lying about her death, and all for some gold. As soon as Brogan learned the truth, he'd ditch her and come back to me."

"Girl, you're ridiculous," Fallon said. "You never chase after a man."

"He likes to be chased," Nisha said. "He enjoys keeping me on my toes."

"I've never heard such garbage. It sounds like he's done everything he can to get you out of his life," Fallon said. "Short of burying a stake into your own miserable heart, Brogan's made it clear that he's not interested in you."

"You don't know Brogan like I do," she said. "He cares for me. He wants to be with me. He just doesn't realize it yet."

Oh, boy. This was one deranged, possessive half-vampire. "Listen, I get Brogan's a catch. He's a hot guy with his own income and is fun to be around, but there are lines you don't cross. You've leaped across all of them and become a crazy ex turned stalker with murder in her eyes. It's a bad look on you."

She bared her fangs. "It sounds like you're in love with him. You need to be careful. Don't trust him. He'll feed you lines and then leave you."

"I trust Brogan just fine," I said. "However, I don't trust you."

"You know what you need. You need to get yourself some hobbies," Fallon said. "When you've got something else on your mind, you won't obsess over Brogan. And he's not all that hot. He's way too tall. And he has hairy forearms."

"I have hair all over me," Wiggles said. "Well, fur. Does that mean I'm not attractive?"

"No! That makes you adorable." Fallon petted his head.

"I don't need hobbies," Nisha said. "Brogan will marry me one day. He just doesn't know what's good for him."

"You aren't good for him," I said. "Tell me where you were three nights ago."

"I wasn't here if that's what you want to know," she said. "I was visiting a friend, nearby."

"Or, more likely, you were hiding in a cave in this forest, waiting for an opportunity to get to Brogan. What happened? Did you follow his girlfriend and kill her when you lost control of your temper?" I asked.

"I followed no one," Nisha said. "And it wasn't serious between them. He's only ever been serious about me."

"Doubtful," Wiggles muttered.

"You're wrong. It was serious between Brogan and Florentine," I said. "He was going to ask her to move in with him."

Nisha slammed a fist into the mud, and it splattered around her as she growled. "I will kill her. She must have bewitched him."

"She was a jinn, not a witch," I said. "And it's a bit late to threaten to kill her, since she's already dead."

"Then I'll dig up her body and... and..." Nisha screamed. "Brogan's mine!"

As Nisha raged and stamped around cursing Florentine, my thoughts turned to Lex again. Had the angels gotten the wrong person in custody? Nisha was obsessed with Brogan. Her temper was fiery, and I could imagine she'd do anything to keep him all to herself.

Was the real killer in front of us?

# Chapter 18

"This woman's out of her mind." Fallon took a step back from the hole. "I don't want her in my forest a moment longer."

"We need to get the angels involved," I said. "They need to hear Nisha's story."

"You think she killed Florentine?" Wiggles asked.

"She's crazy enough to have done it," I said. "And I doubt the friend alibi will stack up when it's checked out."

"It won't. She's been here at least a week. That would have given her easy access to Florentine," Fallon said. "I have a mobile snow globe. I'll make the call and get the angels out here. They can take this foul creature and deal with her." She hurried away.

I moved farther from the hole with Wiggles to get away from Nisha's creative cursing and threats to slaughter us all once she was free.

Once the angels were here, I could refocus on figuring out the next step to find my dad. When Nisha was in their custody, she wouldn't be a threat to Brogan, and the angels could figure out what had really happened to Florentine. My money was on the cursing half-vampire stuck in the mud hole having killed her.

"Now Lex is looking innocent, do I get to have my wishes?" Wiggles asked. "I've been thinking about them a lot."

"Does one of them include becoming Fallon's beast?"

He snorted and scratched behind his ear with a back paw. "What can I say? She charmed me. I don't think you've ever called me perfect."

I petted his head. "I might not say it, but I think it almost every day."

"You could show it a bit more by feeding me daily doughnuts."

My gaze lifted to the sky. "Maybe you should ask your new best friend for doughnuts."

"Maybe I will. I bet Fallon would feed me anything I asked for. After all, I am her perfect steed." He hopped up and trotted around. "Perfect in every way, from my tufty ears to my stumpy legs. Plus, I have three wishes. That makes me super special."

I couldn't help but smile at Wiggles' confidence. "Just remember that saying, be careful what you wish for. Those wishes will have consequences."

"I'll use them wisely," he said, "so long as wisely includes lots of doughnuts."

I glanced at the hole. Nisha had gone worryingly quiet. I walked over and jerked my head back as she flew out and landed on her feet in a crouched position.

She glared at me, her hands and boots caked in mud, before snarling and bolting away through the trees.

I groaned. "I thought this hole was vampire proof." I raced after her, Wiggles by my side.

Nisha was almost out of sight. I slung some spells at her, but she kept ducking and weaving, my magic missing her thanks to her vampy stealth skills.

We reached the edge of the trees, and I slowed as my breath gasped out of me. She was way ahead, just a blur of movement.

I sighed and leaned against a tree. "That went well. Our new suspect in this murder investigation has vanished."

"And it's about to get even better. We've got company." Wiggles' nose lifted to the sky as two angels descended. It was Dazielle and Dominic.

Dazielle landed neatly, tucking her wings behind her. She was followed by Dominic, who gave me a sunny smile.

"Fallon said you have some out-of-control beast in a hole." Dazielle arched a brow, her tone suggesting she didn't believe a word of what she'd just said.

"We did," I said. "And she's a half-vampire with an unhealthy obsession with Brogan."

"Where is she now?" Dazielle looked around.

"She went that way." I pointed a finger to the horizon. "She got out of the hole and made a run for it. We couldn't catch her."

"Do you consider her a threat?" Dazielle asked. "Fallon seemed convinced she was about to destroy the entire village. That's why we came so quickly."

"I doubt she'll do that. Although, watch out if you ever date her and get on her wrong side." I pushed away from the tree. "I think she might have something to do with what happened to Florentine. Have you made any progress with Lex?"

Dazielle scowled at me. "If you call having to let him go because of lack of evidence, then yes, that's progress."

"When did this happen?" I asked.

"I don't have to tell you every move we make," Dazielle said. "Besides, you're his consultant. Surely, he should keep you informed on matters such as this."

I grumbled under my breath. It looked like mean, un-shary Dazielle was back in charge. "So, you aren't charging him with Florentine's murder?"

"It's all circumstantial evidence," she said. "There's no evidence on Florentine's body that Lex had any contact with her. The magic used to pin her in place and knock the wall over could have come from any of a dozen magic using beings. And, you were witness to Lex spotting the glowing creature in the grounds. You being there actually weakens the case against him."

"You can't blame me for that," I said.

"I'll do my best," she said.

I gritted my teeth. "Now Nisha's on the scene, I think you had the wrong person, anyway."

"Why do you think she's involved?" Dazielle asked.

"Long story short, she used to date Brogan. She turned into a possessive girlfriend, and he ditched her when she started talking about marriage.

Nisha's never let it go and has continued to stalk him over the years. Oh, and before I forget, she tried to stake Brogan through the heart during a fight."

"So, she has a temper and a reason to hate Florentine," Dazielle said.

"And, she knew all about Florentine and Brogan dating."

A scowl crossed Dazielle's face. "You couldn't have told me this sooner?"

I smirked at her. "I'm telling you now. Much like you're telling me about what you did with Lex."

"We're supposed to be working together," Dazielle said.

"You're not telling me all the information." My scowl matched hers. "I've got other things I need to deal with. This case isn't top of my priorities."

"I thought proving Lex's innocence would be your top priority."

"Things change," I said. "This one's all on you from now on. I've given you a new suspect with a great motive and a dodgy alibi. You just have to find her."

Confusion crossed Dazielle's face before it morphed into a frown. "You mean I don't have to worry about you sticking your nose into angel business anymore?"

I lifted my hands and dropped them to my side. "It's all yours. Enjoy. Come on, Wiggles." I jammed the notepad into my pocket and stomped down the hill, back toward the village.

I'd had enough of this. The angels could figure out this mystery on their own. I needed to focus on my missing dad and what it meant for the family. I'd been distracted long enough.

# Chapter 19

I hurried past Aurora's store, lifting my hand in acknowledgement as I saw her through the window.

She waved me toward her, but I shook my head and kept on walking.

"Where's the fire?" she called from the door.

My body tensed as I turned. "I can't stop."

"Of course, you can. Come inside," she said. "I need to talk to you about something."

I also needed to talk to her. Was now the right time to reveal what I knew about our dad? There'd probably never be a right time to tell her what I'd learned.

"Okay. Five minutes." I hurried into her store.

"Where are you going in such a hurry?" she asked as she headed around the counter.

"I was walking away from Dazielle, so I didn't thump her on the nose," I said. "She's being annoying."

"You always find Dazielle annoying," she said. "You usually handle it better than this."

"Not today," I said. "What do you need to talk about?"

Aurora frowned. "So serious. No cookies for you today if you keep being so grumpy."

I didn't want cookies. Well, I sort of did. There was always room for cookies.

"Greetings, Tempest," Bandit said. She was curled in a too small cardboard box lined with a blanket on the edge of the counter.

"Hey, Bandit. How's things?"

"I can't complain. Although, I could have done with a second portion of breakfast."

"Too much fruit will upset your stomach again." Aurora tickled Bandit under the chin.

I tapped my fingers on the counter. "So..."

"I'm so happy with Bandit," Aurora said.

"That's good to know." Was this really what she wanted to talk about?

"She's amazing," Aurora said. "She guards the store all night. And I wake every morning to find her nestled on the pillow by my head. She greets me by licking the end of my nose."

"That's not hygienic," Wiggles said. "You must know where that tongue goes."

"It's no worse than where yours goes," Bandit said. "And I have a nightly bath."

"My hygiene habits are impeccable," Wiggles said.

I sighed. "Aurora, what did you want to ask me?"

"News about Lex, of course," she said.

"Oh, that. Well, it's good news for you. The angels have let him go."

"Which means he's innocent." She grinned and clasped her hands together. "We can go on a date and get to know each other."

"Don't be so quick to ask him out just yet. The angels have released him without charge because they don't have enough evidence against him. That doesn't mean he's completely in the clear. He still has a great motive for wanting Florentine dead."

"I always thought he was innocent," she said, clearly not having heard a word I said. "So, who are they looking at as the possible killer?"

"Someone called Nisha Naparo," I said. "At least, that's who I'd be pursuing. She used to date Brogan. My theory is she went psycho ex-girlfriend and killed Florentine. But it's early days. The angels still need to get the evidence."

"Brogan." Aurora tilted her head as she hurried to her bookshelf. "It's funny you should mention his name. I was reading about vampire lineages not so long ago. His family has a fascinating history. The Costins are a proud and traditional clan of vampires."

"Brogan's not your typical traditional vampire," I said. "You don't get many vampires who enjoy running cafés."

"He's definitely a departure from most of the Costin vampire clan," she said. "Wasn't his mom in the restaurant business? He must have gotten his love for making amazing food from her."

"I think so," I said. "He always talks about her fondly. I met his grandparents recently, and they're old school vampire. They even gave me the chills."

Aurora pulled out a book and flipped it open. "I imagine they do. Take a look at this." She handed me the book.

"The Complete Guide to European Vampire Clans. Exciting read."

She wrinkled her nose. "It is, actually. Read that page."

"The Costin clan, believed to be established in 1086. That's an ancient line of vampires."

"That's not all," Aurora said. "That name's often associated with ruthless behavior."

"That sort of goes with the territory of being a vampire." I flicked through the pages. "What kind of ruthless behavior are we talking about?"

"A few hundred years ago, they developed a brutal method of dealing with their enemies. A sort of killing calling card if you like. If someone discovered a victim who'd been killed in this particular way, they knew it had something to do with the Costin clan."

"Not your typical draining of blood and dumping the body kind of revenge?" I asked.

"Some draining might have been involved but not all the time," Aurora said.

"What did they do?"

She leaned closer. "They liked to bury their victims alive under buildings."

I lifted my gaze and stared at her. "Under buildings?"

"Let me show you the page." She flicked through the book. "Here we are. Over a period of twelve months, two hundred and fifty-eight victims were discovered hidden under the foundations of buildings. There's even mention of several victims who'd been crushed by walls."

My mouth dropped open. "Which is exactly what happened to Florentine!"

Aurora stared at me in silence for several seconds, her eyes growing wider and wider. "Do you think Brogan did that to Florentine? He figured out she was lying to him and took revenge using the old family way?"

I shook my head as blood pulsed in my ears. "It can't be him. We trust him. He's a friend. He wouldn't do anything like that. But I think I know who might. His grandparents are terrifying. His grandpa Cezar almost took my head off when we had a confrontation and said he'd do anything to protect his grandson."

"Including murder?" Aurora whispered.

I tipped my head back. I couldn't leave this for the angels to muddle through. If they questioned the Costins about Florentine, it could end in a bloodbath. A lot of people would get hurt.

"Unfortunately, I'm going to have to find out if that's true."

***

"You've got the holy water?" Aurora asked.

I pointed at three clear vials before sliding them into my belt loops. "Check."

"And the garlic?" she asked.

"I can smell her from here," Bandit said from her position on top of the bookshelf.

"Check again." I had both the fresh and powdered kind in my pockets.

After discovering the unsettling history of the Costin clan, I'd spent the rest of the day researching the perfect vampire takedown methods with Aurora. Her bookshelves were chocked full of useful information, and her store shelves full of the things I needed to repel even the most committed vampire from sinking his fangs into me.

"And you've got your light spells primed?" Aurora said. "They won't be as effective as natural daylight, but a full vampire won't like to stare into them. They'll be just the distraction tool you need."

I sparked a light ball. "All ready to go."

Her worried gaze ran over me. "Are you sure you don't want me to come with you?"

"Positive." Aurora wasn't getting herself in the middle of a possibly messy fight with three angry vampires.

Her hands fluttered against her chest. "Maybe you should leave this to the angels."

"First off, I doubt they'll believe me," I said. "And second, I'm friends with Brogan. I want to make this easy on him, give him a chance to tell me what he knows about this murder."

She handed me six wooden stakes as she bit her bottom lip. "Have you thought about simply using Frank?"

"There's never anything simple about using Frank." I spent a few seconds tucking the stakes into my belt loops. "And that's not a great idea. He's been... out of action recently."

She smiled. "That's great news. He's finally getting bored with trying to attack me?"

I hesitated as I looked at anything but Aurora. Frank wasn't talking for a very good reason. Maybe now was the time to discuss the information I had about our missing dad.

"I knew he'd get bored eventually," Aurora said. "I never knew why he was interested in me in the first place."

"He likes to corrupt the innocent," I said.

Her nose wrinkled. "I'm not that innocent. But I'm glad. If he's not causing you any trouble, then perhaps it's easier if you keep him out of action. Besides, you're a kick ass witch. You can handle these vampires."

"Of course, I can," I said. "But about Frank—"

"Oh! Look! It's Lex." Aurora bounded around the counter and ran to the door before pulling it open. "Lex! Get over here."

I frowned. I'd just been about to tell her about our dad. I couldn't do that with Lex hanging around.

She turned and clapped her hands together, her eyes sparkling with delight. "This is the perfect opportunity."

"To do what?" I asked.

"To get him to ask me out," she said.

I sighed. "Don't move so fast. You still need to be careful around him."

"I'm always careful," she said.

I bit my tongue, determined not to say anything about the last guy she dated and how well that turned out.

"Why waste this chance?" Aurora said. "Lex is a desirable guy. If I'm not quick, someone else might beat me to it. Don't you think I'd suit life in a castle?"

I groaned and thumped my palm against my forehead. "Go slowly. You don't need to marry yourself off to the guy before you've even had your first date."

She poked her tongue out at me.

Lex walked through the open door. "Hi, Aurora. And Tempest! I've been meaning to catch up with you. I went to the club this morning but couldn't find you."

"I've been here. I've heard the latest from the angels," I said. "You're a free man."

"They told me not to leave the village, though," he said. "But it's a step in the right direction. They tell me you've been investigating other suspects. I knew I could rely on you to figure out what happened." He sounded happier than he had in days.

"Other suspects who keep getting away," I said.

"Oh! That's worrying," he said. "Who's the new suspect?"

"An ex-girlfriend of Brogan's, but she's not my focus right now. There's somebody else I need to see." I patted the stakes attached to my belt. "Just keep your nose clean for now. This murder isn't solved. Technically, you're still a suspect."

Lex ducked his head. "I had nothing to do with it. I'm still trying to come to terms with the fact my wife faked her death the first time and was then killed in my grounds."

Aurora patted his arm. "You need to take your mind off that. I have the perfect suggestion."

"What's that?" he said.

"Why don't you take me for lunch tomorrow?"

Lex's eyes widened before he grinned. "That sounds like a great idea. Charming company and good food always make me happy."

"Stay in a public place where lots of people can see you," I said.

"Why? This new suspect won't have an interest in me, will they?" A worried look crossed Lex's face. "Do they know anything about my... collection?"

"Your collection is safe," I said. "I'm more worried about my sister being alone with you."

"Tempest," she hissed at me. "I trust Lex."

"I promise you I would never harm Aurora," he said.

I crossed my arms over my chest. "Yeah, that's what the last guy who dated her said."

Aurora's cheeks flushed, and she smacked me hard on the arm. "Lex is nothing like Toby."

"Who's Toby?" he asked.

"Someone not important," Aurora said. "Come by and pick me up at one o'clock tomorrow. I'd love to hear all about your castle."

"And I shall accompany you on this date." Bandit stretched and turned in a circle on top of the bookshelf.

"Oh! That's not necessary," Aurora said.

I grinned up at Bandit. "Actually, that's a perfect idea." With Bandit there, things wouldn't get out of hand between Lex and Aurora.

Bandit nodded. "Of course, it is. I suggested it. In my capacity as familiar, I must be by Aurora's side. I will keep you safe and enjoy a free lunch while doing so."

"I assure you Aurora's quite safe with me," Lex said.

"And she'll be even safer with Bandit as her chaperone," I said.

"Oh, very well," Aurora said. "Just behave yourself, Bandit."

"When do I ever misbehave?"

Aurora frowned.

"It's a date," Lex said. He turned to Wiggles. "Have you decided on your first wish yet?"

"What wish is this?" Aurora asked.

Lex's forehead wrinkled, and he tugged at the sleeve of his jacket. "I have a debt to honor Wiggles."

Her eyes widened. "Oh! You're that kind of jinn. I had no idea you could grant wishes."

He sighed. "And it's something I wish to remain a secret. The more people who know, the more I'll be hounded for my ability. I would appreciate your discretion."

"Of course." She squeezed his hand. "I won't mention it to anybody." She turned to Wiggles. "How exciting! Three wishes. What are you thinking of asking for?"

"Something epic and life changing," he said.

"You're not happy with your life as it is?" Aurora asked.

Wiggles glanced at me. "I wouldn't say that. There are a few things I might tweak, though."

"Let's discuss the tweaking of your amazing life later." I raised my eyebrows and inclined my head toward the door. "We have people we need to see."

It was beginning to get dusk outside. It wouldn't be long before Brogan's grandparents surfaced. I wanted to talk to him before they arrived.

"Yes, you should go." Aurora walked me to the door. "Be careful."

I patted my loaded equipment belt. "I've got everything I need to keep safe. I'm only going to ask a few questions and check the facts." This still wasn't a done deal. Just because the Costin clan had a dark history, it didn't mean Brogan's grandparents killed Florentine. Although, my encounters with them had left me chilled and not in a good way.

After a quick hug from Aurora, I said goodbye to Lex and Bandit and left the store with Wiggles by my side.

"Maybe I could wish to become the first movie star hellhound," he said. "I could star in a series of international bestselling movies. Everyone would stop me to get my paw print and have a picture taken."

"I always thought being in a movie would be boring," I said. "All those hours hanging around waiting for people to say their lines. You'd get bored on the first day and end up stuffing yourself with food from the buffet."

"I could direct a movie," he said. "Although, I wouldn't mind seeing a twelve-foot version of me on some billboard."

"That sounds terrifying," I said.

He snorted. "Maybe not a movie then. I'm seriously thinking about a harem of cute poodles, though."

"And I'm still thinking the apartment's too small for any more animals, unless you want to make a wish to get us a new home."

"I love our apartment," he said. "It's small but perfectly formed. Just like me."

"Then if you want to stay there, you need to rethink your harem."

We walked along for a moment in silence as the dark gathered around us.

"One of the wishes will definitely involve doughnuts," he said. "You could always hire some extra storage for the doughnuts."

"Before you make any wishes, we need to survive this meeting with the Costin clan. Let's focus on that for now. If we live past tonight, we can spend all the time you want discussing your wish options."

He grunted as we picked up the pace. "You really think they're involved?"

"I hope not. I don't want to get on their bad side, but we have to know for sure." I stopped outside of Unicorn's Trough and took a deep breath. "Are you ready?"

"I'm always ready," Wiggles said.

"Then let's go talk to some vampires."

# Chapter 20

Brogan stared at me as I stepped into Unicorn's Trough, and his jaw dropped.

He finished serving the customer at the counter before walking over to me, a puzzled expression on his face. "You going to a fancy dress party?"

"No party tonight," I said.

"You look like a vampire slayer." He chortled as he pointed to the stakes in my belt. "I hope those are just for show."

I didn't return his smile. "So do I."

His grin faded, and his expression grew serious. "This isn't a social visit, is it?"

I shook my head. "We need to talk."

Brogan looked around the café. There were several tables occupied, but it wasn't busy. "Give me a minute to deal with my customers." He turned away. "Folks, I need to close for half an hour. Take your food with you. No charge. It's on me to make up for the inconvenience."

A few of the customers grumbled, but they all left the café, leaving us alone as Brogan locked the door.

He turned, and his gaze ran over my vampire hunting equipment. "You stink of garlic."

"Is it repelling you?" I asked.

"Anyone would be repelled by that stench," he said. "If garlic gets on my skin, it itches."

"And that's all?" Itching wouldn't stop a vampire in a rage.

"It burns if you're a full vampire, but that's not a problem for me," he said. "So, explain why you're here dressed up ready to take down a vampire problem? It must have something to do with Flossie's murder."

"It does," I said.

"Is this about Nisha?" His gaze cut to the window. "If she's back, I can lure her out for you."

"This isn't about Nisha." My fingers flexed, and I resisted the urge to grab a stake. Brogan was my friend, but the tension in the café made sweat prickle on my top lip.

"If you're not hunting her, which vampire nest are you going after?" He scrubbed a hand over his stubbled chin. "I'm not comfortable giving you information on other vampires."

"I'm not after a nest," I said. "But I do want to talk about your grandparents. Are they still here?"

He stiffened, and his gaze went over my shoulder. "Sure, they are. They've just arrived."

My shoulders tensed as I turned. Granny Ana and Grandpa Cezar stood outside the door, their expressions calm and their dark eyes cold.

Brogan hurried to the door and opened it before beckoning them in.

"Why are you closed?" Granny Ana pressed a kiss to his cheek.

"Tempest is here," Brogan said. "She's got questions about Flossie's murder."

Grandpa Cezar nodded at me. "I hope you've discovered the killer. Our grandson has been most distressed by the situation."

"And he's about to become more distressed," I said. "Where were you both on the night of Florentine's murder?"

Grandpa Cezar moved to Granny Ana's side and took her hand. "We were together. We were all out that evening, becoming familiar with the surroundings and making sure we didn't stray into the wrong territory. We already told you we spent time at the stone circle."

"All three of you were together that whole night?" I asked.

"What business is it of yours?" Granny Ana asked.

"Because Florentine Fontaine was crushed to death under a wall. Having researched your family history, it seems your ancestors also used that unusual method of murder to punish their victims."

Grandpa Cezar snorted and looked down his nose at me. "Our ancestors' customs may not be ours. It's true there's a history of crushing our enemies, but that doesn't mean we do it."

I didn't miss the puzzled look Brogan gave his grandfather.

"You've never used that particular method to get your revenge on somebody who's wronged you?" I asked.

Brogan stepped between us and raised his hands. "My grandparents are respectful of the rules when they visit Willow Tree Falls. Even if they met someone who did them wrong, they'd never do anything about it here. They'd deal with the matter privately."

"That's not answering my question." I leaned around Brogan and stared straight at his grandparents. "Do you still crush your enemies?"

Granny Ana glanced at her husband before glaring at me. "How we avenge ourselves is no business of yours."

"It is if you murdered Florentine Fontaine," I said.

Brogan swallowed loudly as he looked at me before turning his head to his grandparents. "We did separate for an hour that night."

"Hush!" Granny Ana hissed.

He shook his head. "You said you needed to make contact with some friends. You left me in the forest, and we met later back here."

"Which is exactly what happened," Grandpa Cezar said.

"And that's all you did?" I asked. "You didn't slip over to Castle Falls and deal with Florentine?"

Brogan shook his head, his focus on his grandparents. "You'd never kill Flossie. You know how much I cared for her."

His grandparents shared a long, intense look.

My hand drifted to a stake in my belt as tension crackled in the air. I jumped as someone knocked on the glass door, groaning as I saw Aurora and Bandit outside.

"Who's that?" Granny Ana studied my sister through the glass.

"It's no one," I said hurriedly. "Pay no attention. They're probably just after a hot chocolate. They'll go away soon."

"Tempest! Let us in," Aurora said. She rattled the door handle.

I winced and shook my head at Brogan, willing him not to open the door and bring my sister into this situation.

"A friend of yours?" Granny Ana arched a brow.

"That's Tempest's sister," Brogan said. "Maybe she needs you for something."

I gritted my teeth. "She really doesn't. Tell her to go away."

"That would be impolite," Granny Ana said. "Cezar, invite the beautiful young woman in. Let's see what she needs."

"No!" But I was too late.

Grandpa Cezar unlocked the door, grabbed Aurora around the wrist, and yanked her inside.

She staggered forward, rubbing her wrist and clutching the purse containing Bandit as she stared at Grandpa Cezar. "Is everything okay?" Her worried gaze went to me.

I caught hold of her and pulled her to my side. "What are you doing here?"

She leaned closer and lowered her voice. "I was worried about you. You're facing down vampires on your own."

"Facing us down for what reason?" Granny Ana asked.

Aurora's cheeks flushed pink as she lowered her purse to the ground and let Bandit out. "Sorry, I always forget how good vampire hearing is. I'm Aurora Crypt." She stuck her hand out to be shaken.

Brogan's grandparents simply stared at her.

Aurora lowered her hand and cleared her throat. "I hope I'm not interrupting anything. Tempest can be a little hot-headed at times."

"As we're discovering," Granny Ana said.

Brogan stepped to his grandparents' side, his features stretched tight. "What were you doing that hour when we were apart? Did you see Flossie?"

Aurora opened her mouth to speak, but I pinched her arm.

She glared at me but kept quiet.

"We were doing exactly as we told you," Granny Ana said. "We spoke to some friends and then returned to find you." She glanced up at her husband.

His back stiffened as he clasped his hands behind him. "Correct."

"What friends?" Brogan asked. "What did you talk about?"

"That's no concern of yours," Granny Ana said. "You should not question us. We're your elders. We always do right by the family."

"Did you consider the right thing to do was murder Florentine?" I asked.

Aurora sucked in a gasp of air, her gaze on the vampires.

Granny Ana flashed her fangs at me. "Mind your business, child."

"I am minding my business. A woman was murdered in the place I live. I need to know what happened."

"Then perhaps you should be out questioning suspects, instead of bothering us," Granny Ana said.

"All three of you are suspects," I said. "My sister's an ace when it comes to research. It didn't take her long to discover your family's bloody history."

Grandpa Cezar lifted his chin and stared at me. "It's a history we're proud of. The Costin clan is a renowned, traditional family. We uphold the values of respect and loyalty. If an individual cannot adhere to them, they pay the price."

"And I suspect Florentine paid that price," I said. "I remember you saying you'd do anything to protect the family name."

"But not that," Brogan said as he clasped his granny's arm. "They wouldn't murder somebody I loved."

"Is that true?" I asked them. "You were happy Brogan was seeing Florentine? Not only was she a married woman, but she'd lied to her husband and faked her own death to get her hands on his treasure. That's not the behavior of someone honorable. There's no loyalty in that. Could you really see your grandson with somebody like that? You were happy with his choice?"

Granny Ana hissed through her teeth, and a growl rumbled in her chest.

"Maybe you should stop angering the vampires," Aurora whispered in my ear.

I shook my head discreetly. This was the only way I would get a confession out of them. Their pride might be just the thing that made them confess.

"That's enough, Tempest," Brogan said. "I trust my family. My grandparents know how devastated I am at losing Flossie."

Granny Ana patted his hand. "We'll find someone more suitable for you. A respectable woman. You shouldn't be associating with a jinn, anyway. They're known for their greedy ways. You need an honorable vampire by your side."

He stared at his granny. "Maybe I'd already found the woman I wanted to spend my life with. Are you saying you weren't happy with my choice?"

Grandpa Cezar cleared his throat. "Let's talk about this another time. Your grandma is always right when it comes to matrimonial choices. She's made hundreds of successful matches over the decades. We'll do the same for you. You'll forget all about this Flossie creature soon enough."

"What if I don't want to forget about her?" Brogan stepped away from his grandparents and crossed his arms over his chest. "What if I loved her? She made me happy."

"Being involved with a deceitful charlatan gave you satisfaction?" Granny Ana snorted a derisive laugh. "She was a deceptive harlot. Flossie was being unfaithful to you. She wasn't worthy of your affection. She wasn't worthy of anything. That was why she had to go."

Brogan staggered back, horror crossing his face. "You did kill her?"

Grandpa Cezar clutched his wife's arm. "My dear, what are you saying?"

She shot him an irritated glare. "I had to act. I'm the backbone of this family. You told me we should wait and see what happened. You said Brogan would get bored with this deceitful creature. I wasn't prepared to wait. What if she'd become a permanent fixture in our family? Our good name would be ruined. Everyone would come to associate the Costin clan as liars, people who deceived and cheated to get what they wanted. I wouldn't allow such tainted behavior to be associated with us."

The exchange between them suggested Granny Ana had acted alone. "You didn't know this had happened?" I asked Grandpa Cezar.

He stiffened, and his top lip curled. "My wife is always right. She has excellent reasons for acting this way. I will support her. You have no proof we're involved."

Granny Ana gave a nod, a curl of a smile on her lips.

"You broke my heart," Brogan choked out. "I loved Flossie."

Granny Ana waved a hand in the air. "It was an infatuation. That's different to love. Florentine wasn't being careful with you. She was misusing your loyalty and using you for her entertainment while waiting for an opportunity to strike against her husband. And she used another man to get inside information on the castle. I know all about her slippery ways. How could you have loved that?"

I glanced at Aurora as her hand curled around my arm. We could both sense how delicate this situation was. Vampire battles were never pretty.

"Florentine cared for Brogan. There was no reason she had to be involved with him. It's true she came to Willow Tree Falls because her husband moved here. She wanted his treasure hoard. And she used Gregor to become familiar with the castle layout and learn where the treasure might be hidden," I said.

"You really think she cared for me?" Pain was etched on Brogan's face. "I want to believe that, but..."

I nodded. "There was no reason for her to get to know you, other than the fact she truly liked you." I pulled the notepad out of my pocket. "I've not read it all, and you can't keep it, but this was Florentine's journal. Whenever she wrote about you, she sounded like she was fond of you. Sometimes, when people meet, it just clicks. The timing was terrible, but her affection for you was genuine."

Brogan's shoulders slumped. He took the notepad and read it quietly for a moment. "I always thought it was real between us."

"It wasn't," Granny Ana said. "She would have taken what she wanted and abandoned you. That is not the way it's done in our family. We find our soulmate, and we stay with them for eternity."

"Do vampires even have souls?" Aurora whispered to me.

All three vampires hissed at her, and she took a step back.

Nice move, Aurora.

"That's beside the point," I said. "You have to admit what you've done to Angel Force. You killed an innocent woman. That can't go unpunished."

Granny Ana and Grandpa Cezar shared an amused glance.

"Angel rules don't apply to vampires," Grandpa Cezar said. "My wife may have acted outside the boundaries of your laws, but the circumstances are mitigating. Vampires take the protection of their family name seriously."

"You committed a crime here," I said. "You killed a jinn. The angels' rules apply to you."

Brogan shook his head as he handed back the notepad. "It's not as simple as that, Tempest. A crime committed by a vampire can be submitted for consideration by the Vampire Council. They will administer justice."

I scowled. "What kind of justice? As your grandparents said, the family name is everything. They could easily argue they were protecting their reputation and making sure your name wasn't tarnished by getting rid of Florentine. That doesn't make it right. A woman's still dead. What's more important, her killer being brought to justice or your reputation?"

"As if you need to ask that question." Granny Ana frowned and moved closer. "Stop trying to twist my grandson's thoughts. He knows what we've done makes sense."

He whirled around. "I know no such thing. All I can focus on is that you took away a woman I deeply cared for. I was planning a life with her.

We were happy together. And maybe, when she'd gotten what she wanted from her husband, she'd have settled with me. I thought I'd finally found someone who brought me joy."

"You mistook lust for joy," Grandpa Cezar said. "I've had my head turned a few times by a rare beauty, but your grandmother always sets me straight. You know when you find the right one. Florentine wasn't it. She was a problem. It's been dealt with, and we can all move on."

"Not until the angels know what's happened," I said. "They're still hunting another suspect. They might charge an innocent person if you don't confess."

"If you're talking about Nisha, then she's far from innocent." Brogan tapped his chest. "I know that from personal experience."

"And you'd be happy to have her framed for this murder by your grandmother?" I asked. "I understand she's on the intense side, but that's not fair."

"Enough!" Granny Ana's dark eyes glinted with fury. "You've gone too far, witch. You come in here, accusing us of a crime, and expect us to give ourselves to the angels."

"You're not getting away with this." I pulled back my shoulders and met her glare.

"And you intend to stop us with your..." she waved a hand at me, "puny stakes, garlic stench, and what I'm guessing is holy water? That might work on newborn vampires, but when you've been around for as long as we have, it takes more than a few old-fashioned methods to stop us."

"I'm hoping I won't have to stop any of you," I said. "You talk about respect and decency, and that's exactly how you should behave. Confess to your crime."

She lifted her chin. "There's nothing to confess."

My fingers flexed around a stake.

All the vampires hissed softly, the note carrying a warning of impending danger.

Brogan looked from me to Granny Ana. "There's no point in fighting. We can fix this."

"Leave this to us." Granny Ana patted his arm. "I dealt with the little problem of Florentine. I can deal with these troublesome witches as well."

"They're my friends," Brogan said.

"And you need have no part in this," Granny Ana said.

I tugged Aurora back a few steps. "No part in what?"

"We need to get out of here," Aurora whispered.

"Oh, it's much too late for that." Granny Ana sped toward us. She yanked Aurora away from me and sunk her fangs into her neck.

# Chapter 21

Icy horror flooded my veins as my brain caught up with what had just happened.

Aurora appeared frozen in terror as Granny Ana growled and bit into her.

"Get away from my sister," I yelled.

I caught a blur of movement from the corner of my eye. A bundle of hissing ginger fur and claws flew through the air and landed on Granny Ana's head.

Bandit dug her claws in as she bit Granny Ana's ear, hissing and growling, sounding as terrifying as the snarling vampires surrounding us.

Granny Ana removed her fangs from Aurora's neck. She kept hold of the back of her head, reached up with her free hand, and pulled Bandit off. She held her by the scruff of the neck as she glared at her.

"Get your fangs out of my owner," Bandit shrieked. "I'll have your eyes out with my claws if you keep hurting her."

Granny Ana chuckled before hurling Bandit away.

I flung a protection spell over Bandit, so she bounced harmlessly off the wall and landed on the floor.

"Go check on her," I said to Wiggles.

He glared at me before sighing and bounding over to Bandit.

My insides boiled, and for the first time in days, Frank inched up my spine. Seeing his favorite target the victim of a vampire was too much for him to stay silent.

Granny Ana glared at me before a smirk crossed her face and she latched onto Aurora's neck again with those long sharp fangs.

I grabbed a stake and a vial of holy water, flipping the lid open with my thumb. I tossed the water in Granny Ana's face. She flinched but didn't stop biting.

I raised the stake and aimed, but she was using Aurora like a shield. If I threw it, I'd injure my sister.

Magic sparked on Aurora's fingers, but it kept fading, as though her magic was dying as Granny Ana continued to feed on her.

Frank roared in my head as his energy prickled the back of my neck. This was just what I needed. An out of control, psycho demon to take out these vampires.

Sweat dripped down my face as Frank's power ripped through me, and I lifted the stake again. Maybe if I didn't hit anything vital in Aurora, I could do damage to Granny Ana. Distract her from munching on my sister long enough to get to her and twist that bitter head off her neck.

"Tempest!" Brogan grabbed my arm.

I growled in his face. "Are you really going to stop me? She's killing my sister!"

Conflict flickered across his face before he dropped his hold on me. "I, I... don't know what to do."

I shook my head. I had no time to debate this with him.

There was an angry caterwaul as Bandit launched herself back at Granny Ana, her mouth open, and her teeth aimed at her neck.

Before she could reach her, Granny Ana flung a hand out, grabbed Bandit around the throat and shook her, leaving her dangling in the air as she continued to drain Aurora.

There was a thump and a muttered curse behind me. I turned to see Grandpa Cezar restraining Brogan.

Grandpa Cezar caught my eye and smirked. "There's no need to fight this, Tempest. My wife knows what she's doing."

"Look away from him, Tempest!" Brogan yelled. "Don't let him get you."

I snarled and tried to raise the stake in my hand, but nothing happened.

"Keep looking at me," Grandpa Cezar said, his voice lulling my rage and stopping Frank from taking charge. "This will all be over soon."

Panic flooded through me as Frank's energy faded. Grandpa Cezar was beguiling me. My limbs felt leaden, and my brain grew fuzzy. I had to fight this. I couldn't let Granny Ana kill Aurora and, most likely, all of us. She'd want no witnesses who'd heard her confession about Florentine.

I tried to pull my gaze away from Grandpa Cezar, but he was like a magnet, forcing me to remain focused on him.

He had one arm clenched around Brogan, and although he twisted in his grandfather's grip, he was going nowhere. He was no match for the strength of a full vampire.

"You stay nice and still and quiet," Grandpa Cezar said, his tone soothing me and stopping my desire to fight as the stake fell from my fingers.

All I wanted to do was sit down, have a big mug of coffee, and overindulge on chocolate brownies. Maybe I'd do that. I could sit here, watch the show, and forget my worries. I didn't even have any worries. I was just here, looking for some fun conversation and good food with the friendly, local vampires.

There was a tiny corner of my mind that screamed the opposite. It was telling me to fight. This wasn't true. Someone was in danger, but I couldn't remember who.

I vaguely heard someone yelping and snarling then something prodded me in the back of my leg, but I couldn't take my eyes off Grandpa Cezar.

So long as I looked at him, everything would be just fine.

Even a sharp, stabbing pain in my calf and the sensation of warm blood trickling down into my boot didn't distract me.

The noise of fighting faded, until it was just a whisper.

A smile drifted across my face as I watched the vampire drain the life out of my sister.

I coughed and blinked, my vision blurring as the café filled with thick smoke that smelled of hot sand and an exotic scented oil.

I waved a hand in front of my face, still focused on Grandpa Cezar, but as the smoke grew thicker, it became harder to see him.

My thoughts wavered, and panic stabbed in my gut. What was I doing?

The café felt like it tilted. I staggered to the side, grabbing a table to stop from falling. Everything snapped back into focus.

"And my second wish is that you save Aurora." Wiggles' words filled my ears, and I shook my head to try to make sense of what was going on.

Save her from what?

I whipped around as Aurora fell to the ground with a muted cry of alarm.

Granny Ana was snarling, pinned to the wall by some unseen force, and unable to move.

I raced to Aurora's side. I checked her pulse and let out a shaky sigh. She was unconscious but alive, but she was horribly pale and cold.

Wiggles bounded over and bounced around us. "Is she okay? I used two wishes to save you both."

My eyes widened as I clamped my hand over the puncture marks in Aurora's neck and covered her in healing spells. "That's what all the smoke's about? You summoned Lex?"

"He's here," Wiggles said. "I used my first wish to get you free from Grandpa Cezar. I wasn't sure what he was doing, but you had a weird smile on your face and had started to laugh at Aurora."

I looked around and spotted Lex on the other side of the café, concern in his eyes as he saw me with Aurora.

A squalling shriek made me wince. Granny Ana still had Bandit in her hand, and she was choking her.

"Wiggles!" I gasped. "Use your final wish. Save Bandit!"

He stared at me in horror. "But... it's my final wish."

"She's killing Bandit," I said. "I have to stay with Aurora and make sure she's okay."

"But, but... I haven't wished for my doughnuts."

I raised my eyebrows. I looked at Brogan, who was battling with his grandfather as he tried to reach Granny Ana.

"Hurry!" I said.

Wiggles stamped his paw on the ground. "She's just a cat."

"She's much more than that," I said. "She's Aurora's familiar."

Aurora's eyes flickered open. "Wiggles, please. Save Bandit."

He grumbled under his breath for several seconds. "Alright. I'll do it. My third wish is to save the stupid cat, Bandit, from the vampire. Not that she deserves it."

Granny Ana's hand opened, and Bandit dropped to the floor. She twisted and landed on her feet before staggering to the side and slumping onto her belly.

"Your three wishes have been granted." Lex bowed to Wiggles. "My obligation to you has been fulfilled."

Wiggles snorted smoke, and his ears dropped. "I didn't even get to wish for free doughnuts for life."

"No, but you got to save your family," I said.

He sighed. "I guess it was worth it."

I petted his head with my free hand. "Go check on Bandit."

"I'll save her life, but I'm not going to be her nursemaid," he said.

"Tempest!" Lex strode over. "What's going on? I had to perform my wish duties before I could do anything to help you. Is Aurora... is she okay?"

I looked down to see color returning to her face. I eased my hand off her neck. "She will be. Keep an eye on Aurora, will you?"

"Of course. I don't understand what's happening." He knelt and brushed Aurora's hair from her face.

"I need to help Brogan restrain a crazed vampire, then I'll explain everything." I raced over to where Grandpa Cezar now had Brogan pinned to the wall. I raised a stake, but Brogan caught my eye and shook his head.

With a sigh, I conjured a huge, dazzling bright light spell, slammed it into Grandpa Cezar's back, and doused him with all the holy water and garlic I had. It was enough to make him drop Brogan and stagger away before cringing into the corner as his skin sizzled.

"How can you turn against us, Brogan?" he hissed.

I conjured more light spells and hovered them in front of Grandpa Cezar's eyes to stop him from lunging at us.

"I'm not turning against you," Brogan said. "I'm protecting my friends."

Grandpa Cezar growled and swiped a hand at Brogan.

My magic would only slow him for a short time. "Lex! I could really use a wish of my own right now. I wish you'd go grab the angels. We've got a vampire who has something to confess."

# Chapter 22

I nudged Aurora, sighing in relief at the sight of large white wings outside the café. "The backup's here."

Three angels descended from the sky. One was carrying Lex and set him down outside the café.

"That's good." She leaned against me, Bandit in her arms, looking fast asleep after being doused in a dozen healing spells.

We stood in front of Grandpa Cezar, guarding him to make sure he didn't escape before the angels arrived.

Brogan stood beside us, his face white with shock.

Dazielle, Dominic, and Jophiel entered the café.

Dazielle strode over to me. "Lex told us you're restraining two angry vampires. What's going on?"

"These are Brogan's grandparents," I said. "It turns out they weren't too happy over Brogan's choice of girlfriend."

Dazielle's sharp gaze ran over the Costins before returning to me. "Continue."

"Granny Ana figured she'd interfere in his love life and remove Florentine because she wasn't good enough for her grandson."

Granny Ana hissed but was still unable to move thanks to Wiggles' wish to keep Aurora safe. She remained pinned to the wall by Lex's jinn power.

Lex gasped in a breath as he stood behind the angels. "These vampires killed my wife?"

I nodded. "The Costin clan has strong opinions in regard to who gets to become a member of their family. A woman who faked her own death, planned to steal from her grieving husband, and dated guys behind his back wasn't one they wanted to be associated with."

"What proof do you have?" Dazielle asked.

"They have no proof," Grandpa Cezar snarled. "This is a mistake. My wife's an honorable woman."

"She confessed," I said. "We all heard it."

Dazielle turned to Brogan. "Did you hear it?"

His shoulders sagged before he nodded. "I did. She admitted to killing Flossie, I mean, Florentine."

"Keep quiet. You're betraying your family," Grandpa Cezar said.

"Just as you betrayed me when you killed the woman I loved." Brogan touched my arm. "Tempest, I feel terrible about this. This is all my fault. Florentine would still be alive if I hadn't gotten involved with her."

I shook my head. "Don't blame yourself. She knew what she was doing. Florentine was playing with fire by setting this up. And you weren't part of her grand plan. I don't know if it helps much, but maybe she even loved you in her own way."

He snorted and shook his head. "My heart's closed to love from now on. I've learned my lesson."

"Don't say that." Aurora straightened slowly, still leaning most of her weight on me. "I used to think that I'd never find love again. Maybe I'm changing my mind about that." She looked at Lex and fluttered her eyelashes.

I shook my head, too exhausted to tell her to stop being a fool and focus on staying conscious, not flirting.

"Have you got everything you need?" I asked Dazielle, feeling an overwhelming urge to lie down and have a long sleep.

"For now," she said. "We'll take the vampires in for questioning."

I grabbed Florentine's notepad from the floor where I'd dropped it and handed it to her. "This could help tie things up. Florentine's journal. It makes for interesting reading."

She passed it to Dominic. "Put this in evidence processing." She nodded at me before turning her attention to the vampires.

I wrapped an arm around Aurora's shaking shoulders.

She stroked Bandit and kissed her head. "That was too close."

I blew out a sigh as I watched the angels lead the vampires away. "It was. Come on. It's over now. Let's get out of here."

It felt so good to be out in the warm sunshine. I tipped my head back and smiled at the sun. "Who'd want to be a vampire?"

"Not me," Wiggles said. "I'm happy to run hot-blooded. All that cold skin and those creepy dark eyes are a right turn off."

I let out a contented sigh. Life felt good again. Everything in Willow Tree Falls was back to normal. Well, almost normal.

"Tempest!"

I turned to see Lex hurrying toward us. I hadn't seen him since the fight in Unicorn's Trough. "Hey, Lex."

"I'm glad I caught you both." He nodded at Wiggles. "I've had a few things to catch up on at the castle since our last... meeting."

"You mean the meeting where we almost died thanks to Brogan's grandparents?"

He rubbed the back of his neck. "That's the one. Anyway, I've not paid you for your services."

I arched an eyebrow. "That's true."

"This is for you." He passed me a card.

My eyes widened. "A gift card to Botanica Magica?"

"Not a gift card, a member's gold card. You can shop there whenever you like and charge it to my account. Whatever you want, it's yours. It's a small way of saying thank you for all your help."

Botanica Magica was an enormous magic warehouse. You could get anything and everything from there, but it wasn't cheap. I felt a spending spree coming on.

"Thanks. This will come in handy. I've had my eye on an upgrade for my demon bag."

He bowed. "My pleasure."

Wiggles loudly cleared his throat.

Lex grinned. "Not content with getting your three wishes, Wiggles?"

He huffed out smoke. "I mean, they weren't terrible wishes, but I never got my doughnuts."

Lex produced a card from his inside jacket pocket. "Perhaps this will salve your grievance."

Wiggles took the card and dropped it on the ground to read. "No way!"

"What did you get?" I peered over his head.

"An annual subscription to Sprinkle's dessert box." Wiggles bounced in the air. "I did get my wish."

"And it's for the rest of your life," Lex said. "Every month, you'll get a box of selected sweet treats from Sprinkles."

"You do know that Wiggles could live a really long time, right?" I said. "That's a lot of cake."

"He's welcome to every bite." Lex touched my arm. "Thanks to you both, I'm moving on with my life. I'm free of my demon problem, or should I say, my dead wife problem. I'm happy."

I lifted my hands. "Anytime, especially if it means more gifts like this."

He nodded. "Enjoy, both of you."

We watched Lex walk away, a spring in his step.

"I approve of him," Wiggles said. "He's allowed to stay in the village."

"He does have a way of getting people exactly what they want." I smiled as I tucked away the gold card.

We walked to Heaven's Door. Aurora and Bandit were looking out the window as we approached the store.

Wiggles instantly started grumbling under his breath and sighing.

"Quit doing that," I said. "I know deep down you like Bandit."

"I'm still having a hard time getting over wasting my last wish on that cat," he said. "I could have had a poodle harem, a lifetime supply of doughnuts, a daily belly rub, a closet of the finest bow ties. No, I get stuck with a rude, up herself cat who's never thanked me for what I did."

"She's Aurora's familiar and has helped her move past Toby and everything he did to her. Sure, Bandit can be a bit smug and self-satisfied, but she's a cat. That's how they're made. I'm sure she'd have used her last wish on you if you'd needed it."

"Of course, she wouldn't," he said. "She'd have gotten a tub of popcorn and happily cheered the mean vampire on as she choked the life out of me."

We headed into the store, and Aurora hugged me. "We were hoping to see you today."

"Why's that?" It had been two days since the fight in Unicorn's Trough. Since then, I'd been catching up on my sleep, doing as little work as possible, and recovering from being beguiled by a vampire.

"We got these today." Aurora hurried around the counter and returned with a large white box, which she presented to Wiggles.

His eyes widened as he nudged the lid off and licked his lips. "Doughnuts! Are these all for me?"

She chuckled. "If you'd like to share, I wouldn't mind having one. They're actually from Bandit."

Bandit stood and trotted over. "Technically, I only made the suggestion to buy them. I don't have any money. Aurora paid for them."

I snagged two sugared doughnuts and handed one to Aurora before Wiggles dove into the box.

"What are these for?" Wiggles grabbed the biggest iced covered doughnut and began to chew.

Aurora nudged Bandit gently with her calf. "Go on. You wanted to say something to Wiggles."

Bandit scratched her ear with a back paw. "I can't remember what I wanted to say."

"Yes, you do," Aurora said. "We've talked about this."

Bandit sighed and wrapped her tail around her paws. "Thanks for saving my life."

Wiggles cocked his head. "I didn't hear that. Say it again."

Bandit scowled at him. She cleared her throat. "I said, thank you for saving my life."

I pressed my lips together. I'd never heard a more forced apology in my life.

Wiggles ate another doughnut. "You're welcome. Anyway, I've been thinking about my wishes. A poodle harem would have been exhausting. And why do I need wishes, when I've got everything I already want in my life? Doughnuts, friends, and even an annoying cat."

Bandit's tail flipped as she stood. "You consider me a friend?"

"How about I don't consider you an enemy?" Wiggles said.

"That's not a terrible foundation," Bandit said. "Aurora, where's my fresh pineapple?"

"Oh, coming right up." She hurried behind the counter and returned with a bowl of cubed pineapple. She set it on the floor, and Bandit and Wiggles ate companionably alongside each other.

"I wonder how long that'll last," I whispered to her.

"I give it a week," she said. "How's everything going with you? Heard anything more from the angels?"

"I saw Dominic yesterday," I said. "Florentine's journal has helped them fill in the missing pieces. She was behind everything at the castle. She definitely faked her death and used magic to make the woman who died in the landslide look like her. It was all to fool Lex, so he'd lower his guard and reveal where his treasure was."

"Even though you're not supposed to speak ill of the dead, that was a rotten thing to do. What about Brogan's grandparents?"

"Angel Force and the Vampire Council are in negotiations as to what to do with Granny Ana. She's admitted to Florentine's murder, but as she said in the café, their Council has different rules from the angels."

"I can't believe they'll let her go without charging her with something," Aurora said.

"They'd better be punished after the effort that went into catching them," I said.

"And Brogan?" Aurora asked. "I noticed Unicorn's Trough has been closed since that evening."

"Gone on vacation," I said. "He figured he needed a break after everything that had happened. He stopped by Cloven Hoof and apologized again for what went down."

"I hope you reassured him that we don't blame him for any of this," Aurora said. "It wasn't his fault his grandparents went all vampy on us."

"He still feels guilty," I said. "And Florentine really messed with his head. He fell for her in a big way, and this is the outcome."

"It's such a shame," she said. "His first attempt at real love and it went so horribly wrong."

I nodded. "And Dominic said Nisha's vanished. She was seen on the edge of the village. She must have heard what happened and decided there was nothing left for her here."

Aurora shook her head. "The things people do when they think they're in love. Let's hope Brogan and Nisha can find their own happy endings."

"Talking about happy endings," I said, "what's going on with you and Lex? I noticed how attentive he was being in the café after you were injured."

Her hand went to her neck. There was no evidence of the vampire bite thanks to the healing spells I'd performed on her. "We're going on a date next week. He's busy with the castle renovations until then. I got the impression he might be moving his treasure again."

"That figures," I said. "Too many people know its location. He won't consider it safe until it's hidden again."

"As if I'm interested in his treasure." Aurora glanced at me. "Do you approve of him?"

I patted the card in my pocket. "I do. His heart's in the right place."

She grinned. "I think he's dreamy. And I wouldn't mind having a few of his wishes. Did Wiggles keep the lamp he rubbed?"

"There were hundreds of lamps in the treasure hoard. Wiggles just got lucky."

"Not that lucky," he said around a mouthful of doughnut. "I used all my wishes on you lot."

Aurora bent and kissed his head before brushing sugar off his whiskers. "And we'll be forever grateful. I could feel my life draining away as Granny Ana sank her fangs into me. It was scary."

"Those vampires were powerful," I said. "I should never have looked at Grandpa Cezar. The second our gazes locked, that was it. He had me under his spell."

Aurora shuddered. "At least they're gone. Things are just as they've always been."

I bit my bottom lip and nudged her gently with my elbow. "Have you got time to visit with Granny Dottie this afternoon?"

"Of course." She grinned at me. "I haven't had my lunch break yet. Why? Has she got a good spread laid out at the cemetery?"

"You know Granny Dottie." I avoided her gaze as I licked sugar off my fingers. "She'll always have something delicious to eat."

Aurora tilted her head. "What's going on?"

I picked up the rest of the doughnuts before Wiggles made himself sick. "Let's take a walk and head over to the cemetery."

"Okay. I'll put up my closed sign." Her expression remained quizzical as she grabbed her purse, tucked Bandit inside it, and locked the store.

I'd kept the information about our missing dad from Aurora for too long. She needed to be involved.

She tucked her hand through my elbow as we headed toward the cemetery. "You're keeping secrets, Tempest. We never keep secrets from each other. Has this got something to do with Rhett?"

"No, this has nothing to do with Rhett."

She squeaked. "Are you sure? Wait! Has he asked you to marry him?"

I groaned. "Absolutely not. Get all thoughts of marriage out of your head. I'm not getting married, you're not getting married, no one's getting married. But, we do need to talk."

Now Florentine's murder was solved, we had our own mystery to deal with. And I couldn't do it on my own.

It was time to get my sister involved in the mystery of our missing dad and see if we could find him together.

# About Author

K.E. O'Connor (Karen) is a cozy mystery author living in the beautiful British countryside. She loves all things mystery, animals, and cake. When she's not writing about mysteries, murder, and treats, she volunteers at a local animal sanctuary, reads a ton of books, binge watches mystery series, and dreams about living somewhere warmer.

To stay in touch with the fun mysteries:

**Newsletter:**
www.subscribepage.com/cozymysteries

**Website:**
www.keoconnor.com/writing

**Facebook:**
www.facebook.com/keoconnorauthor

# Also By

Luck of the Witch
Hell of a Witch
Revenge of the Witch
Curse of the Witch
Son of a Witch
Framing of the Witch
Trickery of the Witch
Wishes of the Witch
Harmony of the Witch
Remedy of the Witch
Gift of the Witch
Toil of the Witch
Jinxing of the Witch
Craving of the Witch
Union of the Witch
Chaos of the Witch
Sleighing of the Witch

If you enjoyed

*Wishes of the Witch*

turn the page to read an extract from the next Crypt
Witch Mystery

## HARMONY OF THE WITCH

# Chapter 1

"Oops! Sorry." A tipsy witch almost spilled her lemon drop down my favorite black top as she staggered past on high heels.

I stepped back and bumped into a warlock. Cloven Hoof was full to bursting tonight, and the only person I could blame for that was Granny Dottie and how ridiculously popular she was in Willow Tree Falls.

Every member of my family was here, along with most of the village and a huge group of Granny Dottie's friends. We were celebrating her turning sixty-nine. Although I was pretty certain she'd been celebrating being sixty-nine for at least five years.

Merrie and Paula rushed past me with trays full of lemon drops, bubbling champagne witch brew, and ginger ice mojitos, ensuring everyone was supplied with drinks.

My chef, Niall, was cooking up a storm in the kitchen, producing an endless supply of tasty nibbles for the dancing, laughing, and mainly drunken crowd of partygoers.

Wiggles bounced past, sporting a jaunty red bowtie, his tail wagging as he socialized. He was always the extravert.

Skulking behind him was Bandit, her ginger tail down and her ears lowered. It looked like noisy crowds and loud music weren't her thing.

I stood with my back against the wall as the music throbbed through me, keeping an eye on things and trying to keep my mind off the subject that had been front and center of my thoughts for what felt like months.

I was still no closer to finding my missing dad. And since I'd now involved Aurora and Granny Dottie in finding out what had happened to him, it wouldn't be long before the secret spread through the village. Aurora was terrible at keeping secrets, and Granny Dottie often let slip things she shouldn't. Once word got out, it would be chaos. Everyone would offer help or words of caution.

A hand wrapped around my waist. I looked up and smiled as Rhett Blackthorn leaned against the wall next to me.

"Hey, Tempest. Are you enjoying the party?" He lightly kissed my lips.

"So long as everyone else is having a good time, that's the main thing." I leaned against him, enjoying the familiar scent of bike oil and citrus cologne.

He squeezed me tighter. "You too. This may be your club, but you should let your hair down as well."

"I can let my hair down just fine. You know that."

"I sure do." Rhett was quiet for a moment. Quiet was his default mode, but I sensed something coming. "What's on your mind?"

And there it was. "The usual."

His soft grunt told me he didn't believe me, but he never pushed. That was one of the many things I loved about being in a relationship with Rhett. That and he was so easy on the eyes and fun to hang out with. A sexy fallen angel in leather, and he was all mine.

I'd yet to confide in him about my dad. I didn't want to waste people's time or get their hopes up that Dad was coming back. I could be searching for someone who was no longer alive. Although that thought made me sick, so I never dwelled on it. The rare sightings of Dad could simply be a mistake.

That was the main reason I'd kept this to myself and only shared it with a couple of people. And if I told Rhett, he'd get involved. He'd enlist his biker gang to start the hunt.

Maybe I was being a coward for not getting more people entangled in this, but what if that hunt revealed an answer I didn't want to hear? What if Dad really was nothing more than a ghost?

"Your granny's having fun," he said.

Granny Dottie was in the middle of the dance floor, shooting silver sparks from her fingertips. People stood around her, clapping her on.

"Anyone would think she was sixteen not sixty-nine," I said. "I hope I age that well."

"You'll be a beautiful older woman," he said. "It's something I'm looking forward to seeing."

I arched an eyebrow. "You're planning on sticking around that long?"

"As long as you'll have me."

A warm glow filled my chest. We weren't an emotive couple, but Rhett was loyal, and I could always rely on him. I should let him in more. I could certainly use more people on my side in the search for my dad.

Axel Shadowsoul strode through the main doors of Cloven Hoof, drawing the attention of several women, who eyed him eagerly as he stood there looking like he owned the place. That guy was never short on self-confidence.

But he didn't notice all the admiring glances. Axel only had eyes for my bar manager, Merrie Noble. He strode over, took the tray she held and placed it on a table, swept her off her feet, and pressed a lingering kiss to her lips.

I shook my head. Axel had always been a charmer and a ladies' man. But since he'd gotten together with Merrie, he'd been devoted to her. It was sweet, but I kept an eye on him, not certain he'd changed for good. If I ever caught him cheating, I'd curse him to a long miserable life as I chased him out of Willow Tree Falls, shooting fireballs at his head.

"I see Dottie extended the party invitation to everyone in the village." Rhett scowled at Axel.

"Axel's a friend. It's fine that he's here. Besides, I thought you two were getting along."

"We get along just fine when he's not using that smart mouth of his," Rhett said. "Ever since he had his little vacation with his father, he's gotten cocky."

"He's always been cocky."

Axel set Merrie back on her feet before walking over to Granny Dottie. He planted a kiss on her cheek and presented her with a huge wrapped gift that appeared out of nowhere.

Granny Dottie giggled before handing the gift to Aurora, who was dancing next to her. She dragged Axel into the circle of excited guests to dance.

"I'll go get some drinks," Rhett said. He strolled to the bar, and I took a moment to enjoy the view. He was a picture of leather-clad perfection. Rhett had a tough side, but when you got to know him, he was a softie.

"Psst! Tempest!"

My gaze shifted as Granny Dottie staggered toward me.

"Are you enjoying yourself on the dance floor?" I caught hold of her elbow as she swayed, her cheeks glowing pink and her teased hair glittering with sparkly spray. Yeah, I so wanted to age like her.

"I needed to get you on your own." She leaned forward and spoke in my ear. "As soon as I saw that gorgeous hunk of yours disappear, I had to grab my chance."

"He's only at the bar," I said. "What do you want to talk about?"

She glanced around. "Any more thoughts on your dad?"

I grimaced. Despite grilling Granny Dottie for hours over her involvement with my dad's disappearance, and any deal made involving my incumbent demon, Frank, she'd denied any knowledge. In fact, she'd been shocked when I suggested she had something to do with Dad's disappearance.

"Nothing new. I keep hitting brick walls. I was thinking about taking a trip to the Dark Realm, see if I can dig anything up." It was the last place any magic user wanted to go unless they had something seriously bad to hide from.

"Noooo!" Granny Dottie hiccupped. "Don't go there. It's a bad place."

"It's the last place Dad was seen," I said.

"If you go there, I'm coming too." She jabbed a finger into my chest, and a tiny sparkle of silver magic shot out.

I shook my head. There was no way I was taking Granny Dottie into a place like that. She was a powerful witch, but she was also my gran. I wasn't putting her at risk. "It's just one option I'm considering. I haven't made a decision just yet."

"We'll figure this out, my girl. If he's out there, we'll find him. He can't hide forever." Granny Dottie adjusted the slightly too tight sparkly purple dress she wore and pursed her lips. "It's just that..." She glanced at the crowd of dancing partygoers.

"Go on, what do you want to say?"

"I don't want you getting your hopes up. Your information sources aren't reliable. A dark magic user and an unscrupulous rogue who makes his money stealing from others. You can't trust them. You can't trust the information."

She had an annoyingly valid point, and it had niggled away in the back of my mind ever since I'd gotten a whisper that Dad was still alive. My two sources of information regarding my dad, Foxglove

Shadowsoul and Isaac Dubrov, were less than ideal, but now I had the idea in my head that Dad might be alive, I couldn't let it go.

"I need to get this confirmed one way or the other," I said.

She patted my cheek. "We do all right, though, don't we? We've been good since he vanished. I'd hate to think you missed out on anything important because your dad wasn't around. Your mom would be devastated if she thought you were unhappy. So would I."

"No! I'm definitely not unhappy. And I didn't miss out. Sure, I missed him; we all did. But I didn't have a bad childhood because he wasn't around." I gripped her elbow. "Don't mention this to Mom. She doesn't need to know just yet. It won't do her any good to worry about this until I know for sure where he is and what sort of mess he's in."

"She won't hear it from me." Granny Dottie pressed a kiss to my cheek.

"Come on, beautiful." Axel appeared next to Granny Dottie and winked at me. "Let's get you back on that dance floor. Your adoring fans are waiting."

"You cheeky boy." She grabbed his hand and planted a sloppy kiss on his lips. "Lead the way."

I chuckled as Axel spun Granny Dottie expertly around the floor, although I wasn't sure who was leading who in the dance. Granny Dottie loved to be in charge.

My sister, Aurora, hurried over, her blonde hair piled on her head and curls drifting around her face. "Does Granny Dottie know about her big surprise?"

I shook my head. "Not unless you've told her. You haven't, I hope?"

"I've not said a word." She bounced in her glittery peep-toe shoes. "It's caused me physical pain to keep this secret quiet. It's going to be amazing."

"And she's definitely coming?" Aurora had planned an elaborate musical evening led by none other than legendary singer Bathsheba Delaware, famous for her magic laced opera performances. She'd sold out all over the world when she was younger. She was semi-retired these days but still put on the occasional intimate gig.

When Aurora had suggested we get Bathsheba to come to Willow Tree Falls, I was reluctant. Why would she want to come here?

Still, Aurora was determined, and after numerous messages back and forth, Bathsheba had agreed to come. She wasn't cheap, though, and had numerous conditions before she would perform. One of which was to showcase her new music next to the stone circle in the village.

"I can't wait to meet her," Aurora said. "I haven't actually spoken to her directly. I've been dealing with her assistant, Charlotte. I think she's Bathsheba's daughter. Anyway, that doesn't matter. Everything's in place. They're arriving tomorrow and setting up at the stone circle at four o'clock."

"I've got to admit it's a great location for a concert," I said.

"I think that's what persuaded Bathsheba to come," Aurora said. "Those old stones have power."

I nodded. The stone circle in Willow Tree Falls absorbed and distributed magical energy throughout the village. It was a big draw to magic users, helping to keep everyone's energy flowing and their magic strong and stable.

"We'll have to be extra careful to keep Granny Dottie out of the way tomorrow. If she gets so much as a sniff of something strange going on, she'll investigate and ruin the surprise," Aurora said.

"I've already checked. She's on duty in the cemetery from noon until nine o'clock. Mom gave her a later shift since she figured she might need a lie-in after tonight. We'll be able to sneak in Bathsheba and her entourage when Granny's monitoring the demons. She won't see anything. By the time everything's set up, we can bring her from the cemetery straight to the stone circle."

Aurora bounced on her toes again. "I can't wait. This'll be a birthday surprise she'll never forget."

"That's the plan," I said. "You don't turn sixty-nine for the fifth time in a row and forget about it in a hurry."

Aurora laughed. "That's so true. Come on. Let's go for a boogie."

I allowed her to drag me onto the dancefloor and lost myself in the throbbing bass and lively rhythms. Rhett joined us, along with a gaggle of other friends.

I pushed my worries about my dad to one side for the night. This was an evening of celebration, a night to enjoy being with the family I still had in my life.

I'd worry about my missing dad tomorrow.

**Harmony of the Witch is available in e-book and paperback.**